This special numbered edition
is limited to 750 copies.
This is copy 485.

REVENANT

A "Nameless Detective" Novella

Bill Pronzini

REVENANT

A "Nameless Detective" Novella

Bill Pronzini

CEMETERY DANCE PUBLICATIONS

Baltimore

❖ 2016 ❖

FIRST EDITION
ISBN: 978-1-58767-493-8
Cemetery Dance Publications Edition 2016

Cemetery Dance Publications
132-B Industry Lane, Unit 7
Forest Hill, MD 21050
Email: info@cemeterydance.com
www.cemeterydance.com

Dedication

For Marcia

ONE

The weirdest damn case I've ever been involved in began, innocuously enough, with a phone call.

I was alone in the agency office when it came in late that April morning, the day being one of the two per week I spend at my desk now that I'm semiretired. Tamara had gone down to the South Park Café to get us some takeout lunch, and Jake Runyon and Alex Chavez were both out on field assignments. So the decision to follow up or not follow up was mine to make, and the subsequent investigation mine if and when it came to that.

The caller gave his name as Peter Erskine, his profession as stockbroker and financial advisor, and said that he was calling from his home in Atherton. The location got my attention right away; Atherton is an uber-affluent community on the Peninsula some thirty miles south of San Francisco. His problem, he said, was personal and "very strange and disturbing." When you've been a detective as long as I have, you get so you can read voice nuances over a phone wire. He didn't sound particularly upset, but there was a detectable undercurrent of tension in his businesslike approach—the way a man speaks when he's keeping himself under tight control.

"How do you mean strange, Mr. Erskine?"

"It's…complicated, and it takes considerable explaining better done in person. Could you possibly come to my home this afternoon?"

I said, "Our policy with prospective new clients is an initial consultation here in our offices, to determine if our services meet your needs. You understand, I'm sure."

"Yes, of course, but this matter also concerns my wife. She'll want to meet and speak with you as well, but her health is poor and she doesn't travel well. If you could see your way clear to driving down, I'll pay you two hundred and fifty dollars for your time, plus travel expenses, whether you agree to help us or not. In cash if you'd like."

Well, we'd been offered more than that upfront, but not very often and not in recent memory. Besides which, the "very strange and disturbing" appellation to his problem was tantalizing, I was not particularly busy, just working a routine employee background check for a large industrial company, and the weather was too unseasonably nice for this time of year to be cooped up inside if you could justify a field trip. Two hundred and fifty bucks plus expenses was plenty enough justification.

I said, "What time would be convenient for you?"

"As soon as you can make it."

"Two o'clock?" I was thinking about my lunch. No breakfast to speak of this morning, and my stomach was grumbling.

"Two o'clock, yes, that's fine. Thank you."

"Address? Phone number in case I should need it?"

He provided them, along with general directions that weren't necessary. The GPS Kerry had talked me into installing in my car—rightly so, I had to admit, despite my general dislike of electronic gadgets— would take me to his home by the shortest possible route.

Tamara came back and into my office as I was ending the conversation with Peter Erskine. Tamara Corbin, my partner and just about young enough to be my grand-daughter. Whip-smart and as organized and creative as they come—literally the guid-ing hand and beating heart of the agency. When I'd first hired her for her computer expertise several years back, I'd been run-ning a modest one-man operation; once she learned the ropes and took on more and more responsibility, she'd worked tire-lessly to expand the business to the point where now we employed two full-time field operatives and another on a part-time basis and were dragging down five times the annual profits I'd made on my own. One of these days, long after I was gone, she'd undoubtedly head up the largest investigative agency in the city.

She set one of two Styrofoam sandwich containers on my desk. Its contents had the warm, spicy aroma of hot pastrami. "New client?" she asked, nodding at the phone.

"Prospective. Peter Erskine, stockbroker and financial advisor, Atherton."

One of her eyebrows went up at that, climbed another fraction when I told her about Erskine's cash offer. "Man's serious, whatever his problem. Could be interesting."

"Could be," I agreed.

Interesting? What a hell of an understatement that turned out to be.

TWO

Atherton is one of those expensive, wooded, hillside communities that prides itself on its scenic attractions and considerable amount of open space. The homes in the upper sections below Highway 280 are mostly situated on large parcels shaded by heritage trees and surrounded by lawns and carefully tended gardens. There are quite a few that qualify as estates, tucked away on acres of real estate behind stone walls, ornate fences, high hedges. You could buy yourself one of those for ten million on up to thirty million or more if you were one of the upwardly mobile, mega-rich folk who'd made their pile down in Silicon Valley. Even the less opulent properties would cost you seven figures on the open market.

The property that evidently belonged to Peter Erskine and his wife was modest in comparison to some of its neighbors, probably worth a paltry three or four mil. It had a whitish stone fence and a gated entrance drive, the gates mounted on ornate pillars and open now. I drove on through.

Half an acre of barbered lawn and flowering shrubs separated the house from the road. Two stories of angular modern architecture, faced in the same kind of whitish stone as the fence and decorated at the corners with red fire brick, the house wasn't half as large as most in the vicinity—no more than a dozen rooms, not counting baths. Over on its right side I had a glimpse of a red brick terrace and, at a distance at the edge of a copse of evergreens, a large hexagonal outbuilding that I would call a gazebo and the Erskines probably labeled a summerhouse. There'd be a swimming pool, too, somewhere around back.

The driveway ended in a white-pebbled parking area that would accommodate half a dozen cars. Mine was probably the oldest and cheapest passenger vehicle that had ever been left there. I made my way to the porch and rang the bell. Rolling melody of chimes, footsteps, a pause while I was scrutinized through a peephole magnifier, then a male voice saying my name interrogatively even though it was five minutes of two and I was expected. Erskine being careful nonetheless, for reasons I was about to learn, before he admitted a stranger.

When I confirmed my identity, a chain rattled and he opened up. He was not quite what I expected, but then that's often the case when you form a mental image of someone you've only spoken to on the telephone. I'd figured him for fifty-plus; he was not much older than thirty-five. Casually dressed in a long-sleeved, light blue shirt and fawn-colored slacks. Well set up, fair-haired, strong-jawed—not quite pretty boy handsome but on the cusp. His unsmiling mien, the tight little muscle bulges along his jawline, confirmed the impression I'd had from his phone voice: man under some pressure and determined not to show how much he was affected by it.

If I was not what he'd expected, either—a conservatively dressed man in his mid-sixties instead of your typical young, mod Hollywood version of a private investigator—he gave no indication of it. He thanked me for being prompt, shook my hand, ushered me in and down a long hallway into a large, bright room with two walls of floor-to-ceiling French-style doors and windows that overlooked the terrace and the gazebo/summerhouse in the distance. The terrace wrapped around to the rear, where I could see a lot of white wrought-iron lawn furniture and the glint of sunlight on water. Swimming pool. Right.

On Erskine's invitation I parked myself on one of several red-and-green patterned chairs. The room, warm from the sun's slanting rays, was decorated strictly according to a woman's taste—the remaining two walls painted a pale yellow, half a dozen whimsical watercolor paintings of elves, gnomes, and leprechauns, lamps with frilly shades, a glass-front display cabinet filled with expensive looking porcelain and pewter knick-knacks. Bright, cheerful elegance, but the kind of room that would make me uncomfortable if I had to spend much time in it.

He didn't immediately sit himself; he went first to the side windows, stood there as if composing himself, then turned abruptly and went to perch stiff-backed on a chair facing me.

"This thing that's going on is unnerving enough to me," he said without preamble, "but it's having an even greater effect on Marian, my wife. Her health is fragile as it is. She's resting in the summerhouse now, she likes to spend her afternoons there when the weather's good. We thought it would be best if I spoke to you alone first."

I said, "What is it that's going on, Mr. Erskine?"

"I think my life may be in danger. We both do."

"You think so? You're not sure?"

"Not completely, but there's every indication of it."

"Someone has cause to harm you, is that it?"

"Not as far as I'm concerned. The idea is fantastic."

"A person you know well?"

"A man I never knew at all. What brought us together, if you can call it that, was an accident. And it was *his* fault, not mine."

"What kind of accident?"

"On the freeway, just over a year ago."

"A year is a long time to hold a grudge," I said.

He made a chuckling sound, dry and humorless. "You don't know the half of it yet."

"Did this man threaten you afterward?"

"Yes. Vowed he'd have his revenge."

"In front of witnesses?"

"Yes."

"Make any threats since? Any attempt to carry out his vow?"

Erskine shook his head. Then, "I thought it was all past history until last Friday night."

"What makes you think differently now?"

"There's no other explanation for why I'm suddenly being stalked."

"Stalked? Are you sure?"

"God, yes, I'm sure."

"Have you been to the police?"

"No. There wouldn't be any point in it."

"Why wouldn't there?"

Another headshake.

"Look, Mr. Erskine," I said, "what is it you expect from me? I have to tell you that my agency doesn't do bodyguard work, but I can recommend one that does—"

"No, no, I don't want a bodyguard. There are weapons in the house, licensed handguns, and I know how to use them. I can take care of myself. I want you to find him, the one who's doing this to me."

"Why a private investigator? Why not the police?"

"Because they wouldn't believe what's been happening, what's behind it, even if I showed them the black host. They'd think

Marian and I were imagining things, hallucinating."

"Black host?"

He didn't seem to hear the question. "You may think the same thing—I won't be surprised if you do. But I swear to you, we're not. I've seen him three times now, Marian twice."

"Seen who?"

The humorless synthetic chuckle again; the muscles along Erskine's jawline rippled faintly. "Vok. Antanas Vok."

"And who is he?"

"Not is, *was*. Antanas Vok is dead. He died in a San Jose hospital a year ago last Friday."

THREE

Several seconds went by while I stared at him. Outside, some kind of bird cut loose with a series of melodious trilling sounds, bright and clear to match the afternoon. Sunlight made golden oblongs of the near side French windows; the places where its rays touched the yellow walls glowed warmly. And here was Peter Erskine, dragging dark shadows into all that cheerful radiance.

I broke the silence finally. "Are you trying to tell me you're being stalked by a dead man?"

"That's how it seems. Marian…well, she can't get over the notion that such a thing is possible."

"But you don't believe it?"

"No." But then he pulled back a little by saying, "I sure as hell don't want to believe it."

"Look, Mr. Erskine—"

He asked abruptly, "Do you know what a revenant is?"

"Revenant? No."

"Supposedly it's a spirit come back from the dead in human form."

"…What, like a zombie?"

"No. A zombie is a mindless corpse risen from the grave. A revenant…" He nibbled briefly at his lower lip, then expelled a sighing breath. "A revenant, according to folklore, is the spirit of an evil person with a malevolent purpose—to terrorize and destroy the living."

I said slowly, "That's a pretty incredible notion."

"I know it. It's Marian's, not mine. She has always had a fascination with the occult. When she was a girl she thought she might have psychic powers. She studied parapsychology, joined one of those psychic research outfits—still contributes money to it. Later on she developed an interest in witchcraft and black magic. Not that she actually believes in such things as revenants, let's just say she's susceptible to supernatural possibilities. Obviously I'm not. Whoever is stalking me is a living person, somebody in whatever nut group Vok belonged to. That's why I asked you here, why I want to hire you. To find out who and why at this late date."

I'd been on the verge of getting up and getting out of there. Over the years I've dealt with more than my share of eccentrics, weirdos, smart-ass cuties, and plain crazies, but Erskine did not appear to fit into any of those categories; he seemed straightforward, worried, concerned for his wife if not himself. As long as he didn't expect me to go chasing after phantoms, I was willing to listen to the rest of his story.

I said, "Let me get all of this straight. You had no connection with this Antanas Vok until the freeway accident?"

"I never knew he existed until that day."

"Who was he?"

Erskine's mouth bent into a grimace. "A butcher. In more ways than one, probably."

"What does that mean?"

Headshake.

"All right," I said. "You've seen somebody three times now who resembles Vok?"

"Enough to be recognizable even at night. Size, height, Van Dyke beard, burning stare, clothing…all the same."

"These sightings took place where?"

"Here, two times when Marian and I were together. The first on the side terrace just outside those windows there, around ten Friday evening. The other time we were having coffee by the pool when he appeared."

"Was anyone else present either time?"

"No. Just the two of us."

"You don't have live-in help?"

"No. A gardener, a part-time cleaning woman, and a full-time cook, but none of them is here in the evenings."

"You say this intruder appeared. How do you mean?"

"As if he'd materialized out of thin air," Erskine said. "I'm not kidding. One second he was there, the next…gone. Vanished."

"What exactly did he do each time?"

"Pointed and stared hate at me."

"That's all? No threatening moves?"

"No, but the implied threat was plain enough. I don't frighten easily, neither does Marian, but the way he looked, his face and hands… Frankly, it made my blood run cold."

"What about his face and hands?"

The muscles along Erskine's jawline rippled again. "They were more bone than flesh. Like a skeleton's. And there was a kind of eerie glow about him. Ectoplasmic, Marian called it."

"Did he speak at all?"

"No."

"How was he dressed?"

"The same as the day of the accident. Shabby black suit and black hat. But the clothing was all torn up, filthy with what seemed to be dirt."

"Each time you saw him?"

"Yes."

"Did he leave any traces behind? Footprints or the like?"

"No. I looked everywhere on the property, but there was nothing to find. Except..."

"Except?"

"A lingering smell. Faint the first time, but last night it was stronger."

"What sort of smell?"

"Nauseating. Like something dead and decayed."

Well, hell. "That kind of stench can be faked," I said. "So can the skeletal resemblance to Vok and the unearthly glow and the rest of it. Stage effects."

"I know. But it was damned realistic nonetheless."

There was nothing supernatural about the vanishing act, either, I thought. With climbable fencing and all the shrubbery and trees on the property, it wouldn't have been too difficult for a man, the living, breathing variety, to trespass more or less unnoticed. Still, there should have been some signs of his presence. Erskine must have missed seeing them in the darkness.

"Where was the third sighting?" I asked.

"Out on the road near the front gate, two nights ago, as I was leaving for a meeting in Palo Alto. He was just standing there, pointing and hating the way he did in the hospital. By the time I stopped the car and got out, he was gone. Vanished, like before."

"The hospital, you said. Was that where Vok made his threat against your life?"

"Yes. The day after the accident, just before he died."

"You went to see him there? Why?"

"One of the doctors called and said he was asking for me. I didn't want to go, but Marian talked me into it. Act of compassion. Honoring a dying man's last request." Erskine's mouth quirked. "Soft-hearted, that's my Marian. A trait I'd always admired in her before."

"Did she go with you?"

"Yes. She saw Vok grab my hand and put that thing into it—"

"Thing?"

"—and heard him swear his sick vengeance. So did a nurse and another man who was in the room."

"A member of Vok's family?"

"I don't know who he was. Possibly somebody from the coven or whatever it was they were involved with."

"Coven?"

"You know, witchcraft."

"Now what are you telling me? That Vok was some kind of devil worshipper?"

"That's exactly what he was. He as much as said so, a lot of crap about Satan being his lord and master. That's why Marian believes the revenant thing is conceivable."

I had another urge to haul my carcass out of there. But it passed and I stayed put. There's a kind of perverse fascination in stories like the one Erskine was spinning for me; the more fantastic they are, the greater the lure to hear them all the way through. I'm too practical-minded to give credence to evil spirits wreaking vengeance from beyond the grave, but there's no denying the existence of devil worship. Or that there are credulous people who buy into the whole occult shtick. Marian Erskine seemed to be one of those, even if her husband shared my skepticism.

"Look," he said, "I know how crazy all of this sounds, but it's true, everything I've told you. A newspaper reporter found out about the threat and claimed to have dug up information proving that both Vok and his wife belonged to a devil cult. He tried to interview Marian and me. I wouldn't let him in the house."

"Did he publish a story anyway?"

"Not that I know of. If I'd seen one, you can bet I'd have gone straight to our lawyers."

"Remember his name? Or what paper he was with?"

"Not his name. The San Jose paper, I think it was."

I said, "Tell me about the traffic accident. How did it happen?"

"Vok's reckless driving. On the freeway near downtown San Jose. I was down there on a business matter, about to exit, when he veered over in front of me so suddenly he clipped my front fender. The impact spun us both around. I was lucky, my 'Vette stayed upright and all I got were some bruises and a cracked wrist bone, but Vok's van flipped and rolled and slammed into the overpass abutment. His wife was killed instantly. They got him out alive but in critical condition. He was barely hanging on when Marian and I saw him in the hospital the next day. Lived just long enough to swear his revenge."

"What was your reaction to that?"

"It didn't bother me very much—just a dying lunatic's delusion. Marian was shocked and scared at the time, and even more upset and afraid for me when the reporter confirmed what Vok was into. But over time, when nothing happened, she got over it. Until last Friday."

"One year from the date of the accident."

"From the date of Vok's death, actually."

"How do you account for the passage of so much time before these recent sightings?"

"I can't account for it," Erskine said. "Marian says the revenant might have had difficulty crossing back from the Other Side, but that's bunk. The only rational explanation I can think of is that there's some kind of anniversary connection."

"Somebody involved with this devil cult carrying out Vok's threat."

"Yes. The man in the hospital room must have told them about it."

"Could he be the one impersonating Vok?"

"No. Vok was short, slight, in his fifties. The other man was tall, heavy-set, years younger."

"Did he give his name?"

"He never said a word."

"Would you know if he's the one who claimed Vok's body? And the wife's?"

"No idea."

"You said something earlier about a 'thing' Vok thrust into your hand. What did you mean?"

The question produced another grimace. "A damned black host."

"That's the second time you've used that term. Explain it."

"Better if I let it explain itself." Erskine slid a hand inside his jacket, brought out a plain white business envelope, then stood to pass it to me. "Careful when you touch the thing. It leaves a residue on your fingers."

The envelope was unsealed and nearly weightless. Inside was a solid black disc about the size of a poker chip. I upended it into my palm. It appeared to be made of some brittle, grainy substance, and there were three tiny triangular horns that gave it the look of a gear with most of its teeth missing. There were also shallow indentations and a shallow piece missing along the opposite edge. Bite marks.

Erskine said, "I assume from your name that you're Catholic, so I guess you know what it is."

Yeah, I knew. It was a perversion of the host, the body of Christ, used in Catholic communion—a black host for a black mass. Even though I no longer embraced the faith, this thing had an unclean feel on my skin. I dumped it back into the envelope, tossed the envelope on the floor. A few tiny grains of black stained my palm; I scrubbed it off on the knee of my pants, kept scrubbing even after the residue no longer adhered to the skin.

"Where did you get it?"

"It was on the floor in the hall Friday night," Erskine said. "Must've been slipped under the door."

"Before or after the Vok figure appeared?"

"Probably before. Marian found it the next morning."

"It couldn't be the same host Vok shoved into your hand in the hospital?"

"Hardly. I threw that one in the garbage as soon as we left the room, for Marian's sake as much as for mine. It…well, you can imagine how frightened she was. To her it meant Vok really was in league with the devil, that he was capable of using the powers of darkness to destroy me, perhaps even to…." He let the rest of the sentence hang.

"To what?"

"Steal my soul."

More supernatural nonsense. "Come on now, Mr. Erskine."

"That's Marian's perception, not mine."

"How does she imagine something like that could happen?"

"I think you'd better ask her."

FOUR

We went out through the side French doors onto the terrace, angled across it and along a wide brick path to the summerhouse. It was as large as a bandstand, surmounted by a dome with little windows in it and partially shaded by a half circle of evergreens; four of its hexagonal openings were covered now by rattan shades. Purple and white flowering shrubs flanked the entrance to a waist-high level; their mingled scents were sweet on the balmy spring air. The structure's position was such that the woman sitting inside wasn't visible until Erskine and I had gone two-thirds of the way across the lawn, and it was only when we stepped up inside that I had a clear look at her.

She was not what I'd expected, either. Something of a surprise, in fact. At least a dozen years older than her husband, maybe more; it was difficult to tell because the dusky light in there veiled her face and upper body. Even so, it was obvious that she was in poor health. Small, frail—she could not have weighed more than a hundred pounds. Pale, blotchy skin. Too-red lipstick that gave her mouth the look of a bloody slash. Hair a dark auburn, expertly dyed and cut. Earlobes heavy with diamond earrings. The smoothness of her cheeks and forehead indicated a facelift or two, but when she leaned forward into a shaft of sunlight I saw dark smudges under her eyes and lines like tiny fissures radiating out from around her mouth.

A thick-cushioned chaise lounge, one of several pieces of wrought-iron furniture that matched the ones on the terrace, was what she was reclining on. On a low table at her side were a cut-glass crystal decanter and tumbler, both half full of what might have been brandy. Even though no breeze stirred the warm air in there, her torso was wrapped in a heavy knit sweater and a patterned afghan covered her from the waist down.

Erskine went to her, laid a solicitous hand on her shoulder; she reached up to cover it with one of her own as he introduced us. The look of him standing there put the words "trophy husband" into my head. Well, why not? That kind of marriage happens often enough among the rich, trophy husbands as well as trophy wives.

Marian Erskine let me have her other hand; it felt thin and dry in mine, like old seamed leather. But when she said, "Thank you for coming," her voice was a strong contralto that belied her fragile appearance. However much of the liquor she'd had, it hadn't affected her speech or dulled her large, dark eyes. Her gaze was steady, direct, without any discernible sign of pain or distress.

"Peter explained everything to you? In detail?"

Erskine said, "Just as we discussed, Marian," and I said, "Yes."

"And you're still here." She made a sound that might have been intended as a laugh but came out as a dry cough. "I was afraid it would all sound so bizarre to a man in your profession that you wouldn't want anything to do with us."

"I deal in facts, Mrs. Erskine. But I try to keep an open mind."

"That's all we ask. You will help us, then?"

"I have some more questions before I make a commitment."

"Of course you do. About my concerns that there may be a supernatural explanation for what has been happening—that Antanas Vok's revenant has returned to carry out his vengeance against my husband."

"Yes."

"Peter dismisses it as utter nonsense."

"That's not quite true," Erskine said. He seemed less in command in her presence, almost defensive. "I have an open mind, too, you know that, Marian. It's just that—"

"Just that you don't share my regard for the paranormal. Well, you're no different from most people." She looked at me again. "I'm not what you'd call a true believer, either, you know—that is, one who embraces all aspects of the paranormal and supernatural without question. I have many questions, many doubts. My interest in the occult is more academic than anything else, though I suppose Peter told you that when I was younger I believed for a time that I had a psychic gift."

I nodded, and she went on, "There are enough documented cases of preternatural phenomena throughout history to have blunted if not completely destroyed my skepticism. I very much want Peter to be right that what we've seen is a living person guised as Antanas Vok, not his evil spirit returned from the Other Side. But until that is proven to my satisfaction, I can't and won't discount the revenant possibility."

I said I understood. "About Vok. You had no idea of his beliefs until the incident in the hospital?"

"None whatsoever. That he was a practicing Satanist and I have some knowledge of the black arts is a macabre coincidence."

"About this revenant concept. Is such a spirit supposed to have physical powers? Could one, for instance, carry around an object such as the black host you found?"

"I can't answer that with any certainty, of course," she said, "but I would think that it is possible. The powers of darkness are considerable, much stronger than we can possibly imagine. Physical objects surely can be made to materialize if not actually carried."

"How would a revenant go about harming a living person?"

"There are a number of ways. One would be to haunt his victim openly, terrorize him until he sickens and dies."

"Like a voodoo curse is supposed to work?"

"Yes, though without such trappings as pins and dolls."

Erskine said, "That wouldn't have any effect on me. You have to believe in that kind of thing before it can harm you."

"Don't be too sure, Peter."

"What are the other ways?" I asked.

Marian Erskine gave another dry cough, reached over to pick up her glass and sip from it. "Cognac," she said when she put it down. "I shouldn't, but it steadies my nerves."

"Not too much," he warned her. "You know what the doctor said—"

"Damn the doctor!" she said with such sudden vehemence that it started her coughing again. "And don't treat me like an invalid child, you know how I detest that." She pushed his hand off her shoulder, helped herself to another sip of cognac. He backed off a step, looking hurt.

I said to prompt her, "Other ways, Mrs. Erskine?"

"Possession," she said.

"Possession. You mean the spirit enters the body of the victim, takes control of it?"

"The victim, or someone else weak-willed enough to do the spirit's bidding. A temporary host, you see? Signified, perhaps, by the appearance of the devil's symbol, a black host."

"If it's the victim who's possessed, then what? How would the spirit destroy him?"

"Theft of the soul is the most diabolical method."

"...I don't understand that."

"A basic tenet of black magic is the belief that the soul is not just the essence of life, but a literal indwelling object—a kind of homunculus that can be seized from within and then taken away. Once this happens, the mortal body collapses and soon withers and dies."

"Is there another method?"

"A more immediate one, yes. By seizing control of the victim's will, forcing him to destroy himself by his own hand."

Gruesome stuff, a mixture of primitive fear, skewed logic, and perverted religious doctrine. You couldn't have paid me enough to buy into it for five seconds. Erskine, either, if he were pressed, judging from the dispassionate look he directed my way from his stance behind her chaise lounge. His wife claimed only academic interest in the black arts, and yet she seemed even paler now and her hand was unsteady as she lifted the decanter and splashed more cognac into her glass. If not a true believer, then close to it—and considerably disturbed by the events of the past few days.

Erskine put a hand on her shoulder again. "Please, Marian, no more alcohol. It's not good for your heart."

She ignored him. Down the new pour went, in two convulsive gulps. The cognac made her cough again, seemed to shorten her breath a little, but did nothing to improve her color.

"Is there anything more you'd like to know?" she asked me. Irritation toward me in her voice now. "About evil spirits, black mass rituals, the Witches' Sabbath, the signing of convenants with the devil—"

"No. That's not necessary. I've heard enough."

She seemed to realize she might have spoken too harshly; she pasted on a smile and said in a more even tone, "What I've told you hasn't changed your mind, has it? About helping us?"

In spite of my skepticism, the conversation had made me feel just a little uncomfortable. Out of my element in a case like this. Once again I had an impulse to back off and back out, but the pleading in Mrs. Erskine's voice, the nervous tension in her body and veiled fear in her eyes, overrode my better judgment. The thing was, I felt sorry for her. And whatever was going on here had a rational, not a supernatural explanation, and that I could deal with. Up to a point, anyway.

"No," I said, "I haven't changed my mind. But I can't promise you results, Mrs. Erskine. It's been a year since the accidents and the Voks' death and there's not much to go on. All I can guarantee you is that I'll do my best on your behalf."

"That is all we expect."

Erskine asked her if she wanted to go back to the house; she said no, she'd stay there a while longer. "Not with the cognac," he said, and plucked the decanter off the table. She gave him a dark look but not an argument, and then dismissed him, and me, by closing her eyes.

He and I returned to the sun room, where he wrote me a hefty retainer check that included, at his insistence, the $250 he'd promised me for the drive down and consultation. I asked him a few more questions while he was doing that, but the answers weren't useful. He didn't know where the Voks had lived. Or the name of the doctor who'd called with the dying man's request. Or the name of the nurse who'd been in the room when the black host was passed and the vow made. And he couldn't remember anything more about the friend or relative of the Voks who'd been there.

On my way back to the city I mentally replayed the interviews with Erskine and his wife. The more I went over them, the more surreal they seemed. Devil cults. Black hosts. Soul-stealing evil spirits from beyond the grave. This was the twenty-first century, for God's sake. Such things couldn't possibly exist in the modern world.

No, but evil sure as hell did. You had only to look at the media any day, every day, for proof of that. All kinds of evil, all kinds of noxious acts. Some of it had touched me before, in various ways. Hurt people I liked and respected, hurt me and those I loved.

One other thing for certain: whatever I did for the Erskines, however far I went with an investigation, I would not let that happen again.

FIVE

It was a little past five when the heavy freeway and city traffic finally allowed me to return to South Park and the agency offices. As per usual, Tamara was still at her desk; close of business to her, most days, was six at the earliest and sometimes seven or eight if she had enough work to keep her that long. Saturdays included, now that she was between male companions. As young as she was, fifty-to-sixty-hour weeks was a punishing schedule and potentially damaging to her health as well as her social life. I'd tried to convince her to ease off a little, to no avail. She was stubborn and ambitious and genuinely passionate about her job. Hell, I knew all about that kind of attitude. I'd been a workaholic myself back in the day.

"How'd it go down in rich folks' country?" she asked when I walked into her office. "Peter Erskine's problem something for us?"

"Not really, but I'm going to look into it anyway. Against my better judgment."

"Yeah? How come?"

"The problem, Erskine's and his wife's, is more than just strange. It's plain crazy weird."

"Crazy weird how?"

"You're going to have as much trouble believing this as I did," I said, and went on to give her a capsule rundown of the two interviews. Right: she had trouble believing it.

"Oh, man! Devil worship? Some freakin' zombie looking to steal somebody's soul?"

"Not a zombie, a so-called revenant. Evil spirit in human form."

"Whatever. Can't tell me you bought any of that supernatural stuff."

"No, but whatever's going on has got both of them spooked—no pun intended. Erskine's the one being stalked, but she's taking it the hardest."

"You think whoever's pretending to be this Vok character is connected to the devil cult?"

"That would seem to be the most logical explanation. If there is a devil cult."

"So why wait a year to carry out the deathbed vow? And why not just off him and get it over with, instead of skulking around at night pointing fingers and smelling like he just crawled out of a cemetery?"

"Good questions. Mrs. Erskine thinks the delay has something to do with the anniversary of Vok's death. Maybe. The skulking and the holding off…scare tactics, to let Erskine know he's a marked man. Again, maybe."

"You really want to go ahead with an investigation, huh?"

I laid Erskine's retainer check on her desk. "Here's one reason."

"But not the only one. You taught me never take on a case just for money unless there's a financial need, and we're so far the black right now we're heading into another tax bracket."

"Chalk it up to curiosity."

"Yeah, the morbid kind."

"And to the reason why we're in business—helping people in trouble."

"Uh-huh."

There was a fourth reason that I'd admitted to myself on the drive back to the city, but that I would not tell Tamara, or Kerry when I got home, or anybody else. Boredom, plain and simple. Nearly all of my investigative work these days was done on the phone—insurance fraud claims, skip-traces, deadbeat dad jobs, employee background checks, arrangements for process serving. Routine, for the most part. And on the four or five days a week when I wasn't in the office, I spent more time rattling around looking for things to occupy my time than I did enjoying myself; you can only do so much reading, and my collection of pulp magazines was about as complete as it was likely to get given what 1920s and 1930s issues of *Black Mask* and other rare titles were going for these days. Mostly I was okay with the semiretired lifestyle, but now and then it grew a little stale, made me feel out of touch and unneeded. This was one of those times.

"So okay," Tamara said. "You want me to run a backgrounder on this Vok character, right?"

"Right. Him and his wife both. On the Erskines, too—anything that might have a bearing on this revenge thing." We didn't usually conduct background checks on clients without a compelling reason, but this was anything but an ordinary case. The more information I had, the better idea I would have of how to proceed.

"What else?"

I consulted my notes. Jake Runyon, Alex Chavez, and most other private operatives these days carry voice-activated devices to record client interviews, but I still use the old-fashioned method of writing down information in a private brand of shorthand. Truth is, I have an uneasy, need-hate relationship with modern technology. There's no question that computers, Internet search engines, iPhones and iPads, GPS systems are useful tools that make detective work and some aspects of life easier; but they're also responsible for a considerable amount of negative change, chiefly the obliteration of personal privacy. The gadgets cluttering up my life are necessary sometimes, but I use them as sparingly as possible. Old habits are hard to break when a dinosaur like me gets into his so-called "golden years."

"Whatever you can pull up on the freeway accident that started all this," I said in answer to Tamara's question. "Also the name of the San Jose reporter who found out about the alleged devil worship connection and tried to interview the Erskines."

"That should be easy enough, if he worked for the *Mercury News*."

"Other IDs, too, if possible: the doctor who attended Vok, the nurse and the other man who were in the hospital room, and the person or persons who claimed the bodies of Vok and his wife."

"Not so easy. Hospital records are pretty hard to access without covert hacking."

"Do what you have to, within reason," I said. "But I don't want to know the specifics."

Tamara flashed me one of her sly grins. "Want me to get on this right away?"

"Tomorrow morning's soon enough. It's five-thirty. Why don't you knock off early for a change?"

"No reason to. All that's waiting for me in my flat is some leftover Chinese takeout and a bathroom that needs cleaning. Besides, I've got plenty of other work to do."

"Not overloading you, am I?"

"Hah. Couldn't if you tried. Only thing I'd rather do is screw, and I can't even do that now that that asshole Horace and me busted up again. Or get next to Mr. V anymore. He went and died on me and I haven't had a chance to replace him."

I sighed and beat a hasty retreat into my own office. I did not want to hear any more about Mr. V for vibrator, dead or alive. Tamara's insistence on sharing intimate details about her sex life, or lack thereof, was one of her less than endearing traits.

#

I did not tell Kerry about my interviews with Peter and Marian Erskine. Most of the time I confided in her whenever a provocative new case had my attention, just as she confided in me when there were interesting developments at Bates and Carpenter, the ad agency where she was now a vice president in charge of several accounts. But not this case.

It wasn't that she would have openly disapproved of my decision to take it on, though she might have questioned the wisdom of it. It would have been an act of cruelty to bring disturbing topics like devil cults and black hosts and vengeful spirits into my home. It was one thing to deal with such matters professionally, where you could employ a certain amount of detachment, another to subject Kerry—and possibly my inquisitive fourteen-year-old adopted daughter Emily—to any of the nasty details.

What I did do, after dinner, was to boot up my laptop and conduct a little private Internet research into the history of satanic worship—as much of it as I could stand to read. The practice had started among primitive peoples in all corners of the earth, I learned, a reverse worship engaged in when fertility rites failed and prayers to benign gods went unanswered. When that happened, some of those primitive races—ancient Babylonians and Druids, among others—appealed instead to the dark gods through virgin sacrifices and other blasphemies.

From the Dark Ages onward, all sorts of sorcerers and sorceresses joined in the Sabbat, or Witches' Sabbath, to perform black masses and attempt to summon demons and make covenants with Satan. Human life was cheap in those days, and in the centuries that followed; people vanished without much effort to find out what had happened to them, especially when members of the nobility indulged in the black arts—human monsters like the Marquis de Sade, Gilles de Rais, Madame de Montespan.

There didn't seem to be much doubt that devil worship continues to exist in these so-called enlightened times. Communicants, as they were called, were still being drawn into witch cults by the freedom to indulge in forbidden practices under the guise of ritual: sexual orgies, blood sacrifices, the black mass communion of drinking of real blood instead of consecrated wine, reading scripture backwards, hanging crucifixes upside down. Crazy shit, as Tamara would have termed it. The communicants were of three general types: those who weren't smart enough to know better, those who got a sick thrill out of sacrilegious ceremony, and those who were addicted to orgies and/or ritual killing. Which had Antanas Vok and his wife been? I wondered.

By the time I quit reading, I was having some second thoughts about cashing Peter Erskine's retainer check and going ahead with the investigation. This case was like nothing in my experience. Grotesque, disturbing. I could still see that damned black host, still feel it unclean in the palm of my hand—a genuine symbol of evil. It was as if it had left a permanent invisible stain. Ridiculous thought, brought on by too much imagination and heightened by my Catholic upbringing, but it lingered nonetheless.

I wrestled with my feelings, and professionalism won. When I make a commitment, I honor it. I kept remembering the palpable tension and fear in Marian Erskine, too—fear for her husband's life, fear of being at the mercy of unknown forces. The one sure way to dispel her superstitious concerns about revenants and the powers of darkness was to prove the threat human by exposing the person or persons behind it.

Still, I had the nagging thought that I'd gotten myself into something I didn't completely understand and that one day, no matter what the outcome, I would come to regret it.

SIX

Tamara had already pulled up some of the information I'd requested when I arrived at the agency the next morning. It was only nine o'clock, so she must have come in early. She looked tired, her dark brown face drawn and the whites of her eyes streaked with faint red lines. Not getting enough sleep. And not eating much or well; she'd lost more weight recently than was good for a young woman with her large-boned body. Overwork, and the second difficult breakup with her cello-playing boyfriend, Horace Fields. But there was nothing I could say or do about it. She was as independent as they come. The only advice from me she'd take to heart was the professional kind, and sometimes only after an argument.

"Not too much on the Voks—wife's name Elza—or the accident that you don't already know," she told me. "The reporter is a dude named Lenihan, first name Joseph. Only he doesn't and never did work for the *Mercury News*. Freelancer for any newspaper or other publication that'll run one of his creature features."

"His what?"

"Far out stuff. You know, weird happenings, unexplained phenomena, that kind of thing."

"Sort of like Charles Fort."

"Who?"

Young people today: no sense of history. "Never mind."

"Well, anyway," Tamara said, "if he wrote up the hospital revenge incident, none of the mainstream print media would touch it. Might've gotten it into some supermarket sheet, but if so I couldn't find a reference through any of the search engines."

"Potential legal problem even if real names weren't used."

"Right. But the good news is that Lenihan also writes a creature-feature blog called

'Oddments' and he posted a long piece there. You can say pretty much anything you want online if you don't cross the libel line. No names in the piece, but there're enough details to ID what he's writing about. You'll see. I printed it out for you."

"Good, thanks. Anything else?"

"A little on the Erskines, yeah," she said. "Still working on the other stuff you asked for. All I've got so far is the name of the hospital—South Bay Memorial."

"What should I know about the Erskines?"

"Not much that I can see. Marian Erskine's estimated worth is around fifteen mil. Inherited money—her father was an electrical engineer, invented some kind of device that he patented and sold to the aerospace industry for megabucks back in the Seventies. She's fifty-one, married and divorced twice before she hooked up with Peter Erskine. He's lasted the longest so far—six years. No children. Long-time member of a group called the International Psychical Research Society; makes an annual four-figure donation to it. Used to be proactive in charity work before her heart attack."

"Heart attack? When was that?"

"Three months ago. Bad one—she nearly died."

No wonder she looked as she did, why Erskine was so solicitous and disapproving of her cognac drinking. Alcohol coupled with nervous tension and undue excitement is a potentially lethal combination in a heart patient. But I wondered why neither of them had mentioned the coronary to me. Too painful and too personal a subject, maybe. And irrelevant to the task I was being hired for.

"Peter Erskine," Tamara said. "Age thirty-six. Born and raised in Los Gatos. No prior marriages. Went to work for a brokerage firm in Silicon Valley straight out of high school, worked his way up to a low-level sales position. Met Marian Erskine at a charity tennis tournament at one of the country clubs down there—he plays and so did she before the heart thing. Not long after they were married, he opened his own business—stockbroker and financial advisor—with her backing. Doesn't seem to've made much of a success at it. Has an office with one employee in Menlo Park."

"He's a good-looking guy. And she's considerably older and in poor health. How good is the marriage?"

"You mean is he the type to put his balls in other courts?" I winced at that, and she grinned. "Well, I don't know, I didn't do any digging along those lines. But if a young guy's not getting much at home, wouldn't be any surprise if he went out prowling now and then. Real careful like, though. Wouldn't want to lose his meal ticket."

"Don't be so cynical."

"Hah," she said.

I took the thin sheaf of printouts she handed me into my office and sat at my desk to go over them. I skimmed through a couple of brief newspaper accounts of the fatal freeway accident. Erskine's version, that Vok had caused it by inattentive driving, was corroborated by witnesses. Vok had been taken to and had died in South

Bay Memorial Hospital, the reason for that destination being two fold: it was relatively close to the scene of the accident and it had a trauma unit.

The background info on the Voks was scanty, evidently all that was available; Tamara is nothing if not thorough. He'd been fifty-two, his wife forty-nine, at the time of their deaths. Both of Lithuanian descent. Antanas (Lithuanian for Anthony) Vok had been born in the Baltic state and emigrated to the U.S. with mother and father, now both deceased, at age twelve, and as an adult had become a naturalized citizen; Elza Vok had been born in this country. No children. Next of kin unknown. They'd lived at 1936 Dillard Street #4 in San Jose, where he'd worked as a butcher for one of the medium-sized supermarket chains and she as a cleaning woman. Nothing on their religious beliefs or alleged cult ties, of course. Devotees of witchcraft and black magic don't advertise the fact.

The printout on our clients contained a few more details, such as Peter Erskine's office address and the name of his sole employee, a woman named Melanie Vinson, but none that held my attention. Joseph Lenihan's blog write-up did.

The header on it was **DEAD MEN RISE UP NEVER?** The tone of the piece was a curious mix of flip-hip—the kind of wry light touch reporters gave to "silly season" stories back in the day—and serious occult-themed speculation. Lenihan's style, I supposed, for all his blog entries. No names were used, as Tamara had said, just terms such as "accident victim of European descent" and "prominent Peninsula resident." Antanas Vok's last words to Peter Erskine were quoted verbatim: "I will return from the dead and destroy you as you have destroyed me. You will die a death far more terrible than mine. This I vow in the name of Satan, my lord and master, with whom I have made an eternal covenant." The passing of the black host was also mentioned in some detail.

Lenihan went on to say that, according to the unnamed "reliable source" he'd gotten this information from, the recipient and his wife were "consumed with terror and immediately fled the room" and that later they had "refused all requests for an interview about the incident." He then wrote: "Subsequent investigation revealed undeniable evidence that the dead man worshipped the devil and took part in satanic rituals and blow-your-mind sex orgies." And finished up with: "Is it possible that a dead dude in league with Lucifer can wreak vengeance on the living? Only time will tell."

Assuming the Vok quote was accurate, and it probably was since Lenihan also knew about the black host, the "reliable source" had to be somebody who was in the hospital room at the time. The nurse Erskine had mentioned? Or had Lenihan managed to track down the tall, heavy-set, stoic party related to or acquainted with the Voks?

The "undeniable evidence" verifying the devil worship was given as "a bone-freezing collection of grimoires, drawings of pentagrams and other black magic symbols, correspondence describing blood sacrifices, and other weird deSade type stuff." Some of the titles of the grimoires, or manuals for invoking demons and spirits of the dead, were listed: *Malleus Maleficarum. The Golden Bough. The Book of Eibon. The Grimoire of Pope Honorius*. And two in German, which apparently Vok had been conversant in: *Die Walpurgisnacht im Westphalialeben* and *Den Nederwelt von Renaissanischer Zeit.*

How Lenihan knew all this wasn't stated, though there was a sly inference that he'd managed to gain access to the couple's apartment after Vok's death, just long enough to view its contents and take some notes. Whether he'd also appropriated any of the books or other items was an unanswered question. He did say that all of the evidence "mysteriously disappeared shortly afterward," the inference there being that he'd gone back for a second look and found the apartment cleaned out.

That was all. Anything more I would have to try to pry out of Lenihan himself. If I could get him to talk to me in the first place.

The address Tamara had found for him was in Santa Clara, north of San Jose; she'd also gotten his telephone number. A page of background info told me he was forty years old, unmarried, and—no surprise—a pothead with one arrest for possession, another plus a hand-slap conviction for minor dealing. Writing creature features was apparently an avocation; his main source of income came from repairing computers for college students and others who couldn't afford topline service, work he did from home.

I pulled the desk phone over and tapped out his number. The voice that answered said, "Lenihan's Service, at your service," in a slow and mellow drawl, as if he might already be a little stoned.

I gave him my name, nothing more, and asked if he'd be home for the next couple of hours. He said, "No plans to go anywhere. Computer problem? I specialize in pcs, but I do Macs, too."

"We can discuss the problem when I get there. Hour, hour and fifteen minutes okay?"

"Any time. I'll be here."

SEVEN

Santa Clara is another upscale South Bay community, not as affluent as Atherton but still a desirable nesting place for what's left of the upper middle class. It's also the new home of what used to be the San Francisco 49ers. I say used to be because many of the homegrown city dwellers like me who loyally supported the team at Kezar and Candlestick for decades were none too happy with the move forty-three miles south to the glitzy new, super expensive Levi's stadium—a stadium that could have and should have been built on available city land next to AT&T Park in downtown S.F.

Sure, winning the bid to host the 2016 Super Bowl was a major coup for the organization and a financial boon for San Francisco despite the South Bay location of the game. But that's not enough to mollify me and many of the other faithful in the city and the North Bay. If anything, it makes the move seem even more of a defection, a fan-base shift that amounts to a collective slap in the face of the old guard. As far as we're concerned, the ownership should be forced to drop "San Francisco" from the team name and replace it with something generic and more honest—the Golden State 49ers, for instance, following the lead of the pro basketball franchise when the Warriors quit playing their games in the city back in 1971.

As fashionable as most of Santa Clara is, it has its pockets of lower income housing. Joe Lenihan lived in one of these, in a nondescript apartment house not far off the 101 freeway. His unit was on the second floor, rear. I rang his bell, identified myself when his voice came over the intercom, and he said, "Come on up, door's open," and buzzed me in.

The front section of what was probably his apartment's living room had been turned into a kind of business anteroom by the addition of wall-to-wall blue curtains. The space was crammed with two tables and two chairs facing each other across the larger table. A couple of desktop pcs and a laptop wearing nametags sat on the smaller table, evidently repaired and awaiting customer pick-up.

A couple of seconds after I entered, the curtains parted and I had my first look at Joe Lenihan. He wasn't what I'd expected any more than Peter Erskine had been. The image I'd had was of a bearded, somewhat scruffy neo-hippie reeking of pot smoke. He was the antithesis of that: clean-shaven, with gray-flecked brown hair trimmed short and clear hazel eyes; dressed in a loose sport shirt and corduroys that were old and somewhat frayed but clean. And not even a stray whiff of marijuana came from him or from behind the curtains. You'd think that at my age and as many years as I've been in business, I would know better than anyone not to fall into the preconceived-notion trap.

He had a welcoming smile for me, but it dimmed somewhat when he saw that my hands were empty. "No computer? I don't sell them, you know, just repair them." I'd been wrong about his voice, too: slow and mellow was apparently his natural way of speaking.

"Computers isn't the reason I'm here, Mr. Lenihan."

"No?" His expression brightened again. "You wouldn't be connected with the media, would you? Come to offer me a writing gig?"

"Sorry, no," I said, and then lied a little. "But I've read your blog."

"Well, one of the chosen few. A pleasure." The smile tilted a little, self-deprecatingly. "Assuming you don't have a complaint about one of my entries, that is."

"No complaints. Just some questions about a particular piece you wrote last year."

"Which one?"

"The one called 'Dead Men Rise Up Never?' About the devil worshipping accident victim and his deathbed vow."

"Oh, sure. Real weird true story. What about it?"

"I'd like some information on your sources."

Lenihan had beetling brows; one of them arched upward into a boomerang shape over a narrowed eye. The upcurve of his mouth was wary now. "Why? After all this time?"

"Professional reasons." I showed him the photostat of my license.

The other eyebrow humped up to make two boomerangs. The smile stayed, the wariness vanished. "No shit," he said in a pleased sort of way. "How come a private eye's interested in devil worshippers?"

"Not that per se, just Antanas Vok and the cult he belonged to."

"Antanas Vok. So you know his name." Then, eagerly, "Why do you want to know my sources? Who're you working for?"

"That's confidential."

"The guy in Atherton? Did something happen to him?"

"Confidential."

"Yeah, well, so are my sources." Pause. "But maybe we could work something out. What's in it for me if I tell you?"

"Satisfaction in helping solve the problem I'm investigating."

"Hah."

"All right. How about twenty bucks?"

"Well, I can always use extra cash," Lenihan said, "but I can use a good story more. Maybe you don't know it, but I'm kind of a jack of all trades. Freelance journalist as well as blogger and computer repairman."

"Uh-huh. But all I can let you have is the twenty."

"Not even a little something I can build a story on?"

"Not even a hint."

He thought it over, nibbling on a corner of his lower lip. Pretty soon he said, "Well, what the hell. Make it fifty bucks and you've got a deal."

"Fifty's a little steep."

"Not for what I have to tell you."

"All right, done." I could afford not to quibble; the money would come out of Peter Erskine's pocket eventually, not mine. I took two twenties and a ten from my wallet and laid them on the table between us, but I kept my hand on the bills when Lenihan reached for them. "After you've told me and I'm sure you're being straightforward."

"Hey," he said, and now he sounded wounded and put-upon, "one thing I don't do is lie for personal gain. Not even to my friends."

"Good for you. Who told you about Vok's vow of vengeance?"

"The nurse who was in the room at the time. Ellen Bowers."

"Why did she confide in you?"

"We hook up now and then, Ellen and me. She knows I'm into the world of weird and this Vok thing was right up my alley." A sly grin. "I showed her my appreciation with dinner and a good fuck."

My reaction to that was an expressionless stare, to let him know I was not going to play the see-what-a-stud-I-am-wink-wink game. "What did she have to say about the other man in the room? You didn't mention him in your blog piece."

"What other man?"

"Relative or friend of Vok's, apparently."

"Yeah? Well, I can't help you there. Ellen never mentioned anybody else being in the room."

"Sure about that?"

"Positive. I'd've put it into the write-up if she had."

"Did you ask her who claimed the bodies of Vok and his wife?"

"Nobody claimed them."

"Oh?"

"Ellen checked for me," Lenihan said. "No next of kin located and nobody else came forward. Both bodies planted at county expense."

I mulled that over for a few seconds before I asked, "Did you turn up any names in the Voks' apartment—other individuals who might be involved in this cult they belonged to?"

"Ah…I can't answer that."

"No? Why not?"

He looked a little sheepish now. "Well, the truth is, I went there but the place was locked up tight and I couldn't convince the building manager to let me in."

"Then how did you find out about the books and the other black arts stuff the Voks had?"

"I didn't." The grin again, and a shrug. "Details make for a better story, whether they've been confirmed or not. Poetic license, you know?"

"Meaning you made up that part of it?"

"Well, not completely. The grimoires I listed are all genuine volumes, and I figured there were bound to be pentagrams and other shit linking the Voks to a devil cult."

Some journalist. "But you don't know that there was."

"No. But Vok admitted to Satan being his lord and master. Pact with the devil, right?"

"That doesn't mean it's true," I said. "He was dying, angry, probably not in his right mind."

"You're forgetting the black host. Ellen saw him shove it into the guy's hand. The wife nearly freaked when she saw it, so it must've been genuine. That and the vow makes Vok a devil worshipper in my book."

But not in mine, not necessarily. "Does Ellen Bowers still work at South Bay Memorial?"

"Yep."

"On duty today, would you know?"

He shook his head. "We're not that close."

"But you do have the hospital's phone number?"

"Sure. Ellen's, too, if you want it."

"Both."

"Do I get the fifty bucks then?"

I told him yes, and he said he'd have to get the numbers from his cell. He went away through the curtains, came back pretty soon with them scrawled on a piece of notepaper. When I took my hand off the bills, he made them disappear as if by a little magic trick of his own.

He grinned again. "Nice doing business with you," he said. "Hope you find what you're looking for."

I didn't answer him, or return his salute as I turned to leave. I may have to deal with people who have shoddy morals and ethics, and who think nothing of cavalierly adding to the misinformation on the Internet, but I don't have to be polite to them.

EIGHT

In the car I called South Bay Memorial to find out if Ellen Bowers was on duty today. She was, but currently assisting on a surgery and unavailable until after two o'clock. So I programmed the Voks' former address, 1936 Dillard Street, into the GPS and let the thing guide me down 101 into San Jose.

The address was in one of the poorer parts of the city, a mixed neighborhood with Hispanics dominating. The building was a somewhat rundown, six-unit apartment house flanked by a bodega on one side, another apartment building on the other. Cooking odors old and new clogged the air in the narrow foyer. Pasted above the name Rodriguez on the mailbox for apartment #1 was an old Dymo Label with the word Manager on it. I pushed the bell, waited, pushed it again. Just as I was about to try for a third and last time, the intercom crackled and a voice said, "Yeah? What is it?" The crackling was so bad I barely understood the words, and couldn't tell if the voice was male or female.

I gave my name and said I was there on a business matter, but none of it got through to whoever was on the other end. There was some staticky chatter that I couldn't understand at all; another attempt on my part didn't get through, either. The intercom shut off, and a few seconds later the door to a ground floor apartment popped open and a guy in an armless undershirt came out. He peered through the front door glass at me, yanked it open, and snapped irritably, "Goddamn thing don't never work right," as if the intercom's failings were my fault. "What you want? Selling something, we don't want it."

"I'm not a salesman. You're Mr. Rodriguez?"

"I asked you what you want."

"To talk to the manager. Is that you?"

"No, my wife, but she's at work." He didn't say why he wasn't also at work, but then maybe he had a night job. And a tolerant employer, if so, since he reeked of beer. "No empty units, if that's what you're looking for."

"It's not. What I'm looking for is some information on a couple who lived here over a year ago. The Voks—Antanas and Elza Vok."

"Them two." Rodriguez scowled at me. He was a big guy, forty or so, with hairy arms and chest and a hanging beer gut that hid the belt buckle on his trousers. "They're dead, killed in a car smash. Why you want to know about them?"

"I'm trying to locate their next of kin."

"Why? What for?"

"Can you help me, Mr. Rodriguez?"

"No. I mind my own business, man. Besides, them other guys was pretty damn creepy."

"What other guys?"

"The two come around here and took some of the Voks' stuff away."

"When was this? How soon after the car smash?"

"Morning after he died in the hospital."

Fast work, if Rodriguez's memory was accurate. The kind that suggests urgency and purpose.

"Can you describe the men?" I asked.

"After a year? Come on, man."

"I'd appreciate it if you'd try to remember."

He didn't have to try very hard; he remembered them, all right. Pretty soon he said, "One was like the Voks. You know, foreign."

"Lithuanian?"

A fat shoulder lifted, dropped again.

"What about the other one?"

"White guy. Butt ugly, built like an ox. They wasn't the painting brothers, that's for sure."

"Painting brothers?"

"Yeah. Sign on the door of the van they had."

"The Painting Brothers, that was the company name?"

"No, no. The brothers' name was the same as that guy used to be on late-night TV. The talk show guy."

"I don't watch late-night TV."

"Leno, man. L-e-n-o. Leno Brothers Painting."

"Do you recall where the business was located?"

"Nah. My memory ain't that good."

"How old would you say the two men were?"

"Not as old as the Voks. I didn't look at them too close. Creepy, like I said."

"In what way?"

"Just creepy," Rodriguez said. "You know how you meet somebody, strangers, you get these vibes tell you you don't want to have nothing to do with them? Like that."

"Were you the one who let them into the Voks' apartment?"

"Not me. My wife took 'em up."

"How did you and she know they were authorized to remove the Voks' belongings?"

"They had a paper."

"What kind of paper?"

Another shrug. "Maria was okay with it. Didn't think they was as creepy as I did… ain't nothing much bothers her. Anyway, why should we care? Sooner they got the stuff out, sooner we could rent the unit again. The owner don't like empty apartments."

"Did they take everything the Voks' owned?"

"Left the furniture," Rodriguez said. "Clothes, too. Crappy stuff, all of it. We had to dump the clothes at Goodwill. But not the furniture—new renters didn't have none of their own, and they didn't care it was crappy."

"What exactly did the men haul away?"

"Cartons full of stuff. Took 'em a couple of hours."

"Any idea what was in the cartons?"

Shrug. "Don't know, don't care."

"Were you or your wife ever in the apartment when the Voks lived in it?"

"Hell, no. They didn't want nobody in there. Kept to themselves, never had much to say."

"Did they have many visitors?"

"Not that I seen. Never paid no attention." Rodriguez belched beerily and squinted down his nose at me. "Hey, all these questions. How come you want to know so much about the Voks?"

"I told you, I'm trying to track down their next of kin."

"Yeah, well, you come to the wrong place, man." He belched again. "I got no more time to talk. Things to do inside."

Like open another beer. "Thanks for your time, Mr. Rodriguez. *Buenas tardes.*"

"Yeah," he said, and backed up and shut the door in my face.

NINE

I looked up Leno Brothers Painting on my trusty new iPhone. Just about every business has a website these days, and this outfit was no exception. They were located in Campbell, a small city adjacent to San Jose on the west. The two brothers were Floyd and Harvey and there were photographs of each on the site; the one named Harvey appeared to qualify as "butt ugly, built like an ox." They evidently ran a cut-rate outfit with emphasis on speed rather than quality of work. "Nobody Beats Our Prices. Fastest Brushes in the West."

The address turned out to be in an industrial area not far off Highway 17. Narrow piece of property sandwiched between an outfit that sold solenoid valves and a plumbing supply company's pipe yard. The building's exterior was neither rundown nor prosperous looking—just a small, nondescript blue collar business like thousands of others. A none too clean white van sat in the driveway alongside, facing the street.

An overhead bell rang a couple of off-key notes when I entered. The interior, unoccupied at the moment, wasn't much to look at either. There was a linoleum-topped counter with some paint-sample books on it, a stack of gallon cans with a placard propped against them that had the words **Sale—Big Savings** written on it, and walls adorned with photographs of freshly painted houses by way of advertisement for the Leno brothers' handiwork.

Beyond the counter was an areaway that apparently led to a workroom and storage area at the rear. A man wearing a stained white smock and painters' cap appeared there and walked up to the counter, wiping his hands on a large rag, not quite hurrying. The Leno named Floyd—smaller, leaner, and older than his brother, craggy faced, eyes the shiny color of black olives. His forehead, under a thatch of thinning, dust-colored hair, was oddly crosshatched with a pattern of lines that resembled nothing so much as a tic-tac-toe drawing.

"Yes, sir? Help you?"

"Mr. Leno?"

"Floyd Leno, that's right."

Under normal circumstances I would have showed him ID and come straight to the point of my visit, as I'd done with Lenihan and Rodriguez. But these were not normal circumstances. So I played a role instead.

"I'm not here about a painting job or anything like that," I said, making my voice hesitant and a little nervous, as if I were unsure of myself. "I…well, I understand you knew a man named Vok."

"Who?"

"Vok. Antanas Vok."

You had to be paying close attention to see the change in his eyes, like shutters coming down over a pair of tiny windows. Otherwise his expression remained the same. "Name's not familiar. Customer of ours?"

"I don't think so, no. I thought he must be…well, a good friend of you and your brother."

"Why would you think that?"

"On account of your brother and another friend cleaned out the Voks' apartment after they were killed in that accident last year."

He looked at me steadily while he did some more hand-wiping; the rag smelled strongly of turpentine. "Who told you that?"

"Tenant in the building where they used to live."

"He made a mistake," Leno said. "I told you, I don't know anybody named Vok."

"But maybe your brother does. Is he here?"

"Out on a job. What's your interest in this Vok anyway?"

I cleared my throat before I said, "I met him where he used to work, not long before he was killed. We had a talk one night."

"Talk about what?"

"About this…group he belonged to."

"What kind of group?"

"People who believe in doing things other people wouldn't approve of. It sounded like something I'd like try, but I…I guess I wasn't ready at the time. And then there was the accident and Vok hadn't given me the names of anybody else in the group, so I tried to forget about it. But I couldn't. Things haven't been going too well for me lately, and now…well, I'm ready for a change, a new way of living the rest of my life."

"I don't know what you're talking about, mister."

"You sure? I mean, I'm serious about wanting to get into this group. Real serious. I've got a little money saved, if that's what it takes…."

Apparently it wasn't. "You're not making any sense," he said. There was a cold steel edge in his voice now. The black eyes no longer seemed shuttered; they were fixed on me in a glazed, unblinking stare, like that of a corpse. "And you're wasting my time, I got work to do. Go peddle your bullshit someplace else."

"It's not bullshit—"

"It is to me. You know what's good for you, mister, you won't come around here anymore. My brother's got even less patience than me, and a mean temper when he's bugged for no reason."

"Are you...threatening me?"

"Call it friendly advice," Leno said. He threw the smelly rag down on the counter, gestured at the door. "On your way."

Bust. Maybe I hadn't played the role well enough. Maybe Leno and his brother weren't involved in a devil cult after all. Maybe, if they were, the cult wasn't taking in new communicants. Or maybe in order to join you had to be sponsored by one of the members, to ensure complete secrecy.

Too many maybes. Unless Tamara could turn up something useful on the Leno brothers, what they amounted to was a dead end.

TEN

I don't like hospitals.

My antipathy isn't as strong as Jake Runyon's—he spent long months watching his second wife die of ovarian cancer in a Seattle hospital—but it's strong enough. I've been inside one or another too damn often, as patient and visitor both, the last time in Placerville on a two-day vigil after Kerry's kidnap ordeal, praying for her to pull out of a semi-coma. There's nothing worse than seeing someone you love hooked up to machines and IVs, dying or perilously close to it. No one who has gone through that can ever be comfortable in a hospital again, even on the kind of brief professional mission that took me to South Bay Memorial. I could feel myself tightening up, my pulse rate jump, as soon as I walked through the door into the main lobby. Health care facility. Right. The sooner I got this visit over with, the better *my* health care would be.

I told the woman staffing the Information Desk that I wanted to speak with Nurse Ellen Bowers on a personal matter. She checked a list, made a call, and then directed me to the nurses' station on the third floor. Two nurses up there, one of each sex; the woman wasn't Ellen Bowers. Ms. Bowers was "on her rounds," the male nurse told me, and expected back shortly.

There were some chairs in a small waiting area, one of which I was invited to occupy. So I sat there and did what I could to block out the hospital sounds and smells by ruminating on the Rodriguez and Floyd Leno interviews.

Harvey Leno and an unidentified Lithuanian, with a paper allegedly authorizing the removal of the Voks' personal belongings. Why in such a hurry? There could be an innocent cultural explanation, if the Lithuanian was a friend or close relative. It also could have something to do with the nature of those belongings, if Lenihan had been closer to the truth than he realized in his made-up description of the apartment's black arts-related contents. No way now that I could see, after the Leno blow-off, of finding out which.

I'd been waiting there seven or eight minutes when Ellen Bowers returned to the station. I hadn't let myself form any pre-conceived notions about what she'd be like, and it was just as well. There was nothing particularly memorable about her unless you were a man attracted to large-breasted women—Lenihan's preference, no doubt. Late thirties, wheat-blond hair, a little on the plump side. Large gray eyes, the irises rimmed in black—her best feature. A pleas-antly quizzical smile took on a sardonic edge when I introduced myself and told her how I'd gotten her name.

"My good friend Joe," she said, as if he were anything but. "What did he tell you about me?"

"About you personally? Nothing." I was not about to repeat Lenihan's uncalled-for sexual comment. "Just that you were the source of an article he wrote for his blog about a year ago, concerning an accident victim named Antanas Vok."

"Oh...that. Is that why you're here? I thought maybe Joe told you I..." She didn't finish the sentence, but I had a pretty good idea what she'd been about to say. If Lenihan bragged about her as an easy score to others as casually as he had to a stranger like me, he was an even bigger schmuck than I'd taken him for.

"You were present when Vok delivered his vengeance threat, is that right?"

"Yes, I was there, and I wish to God I hadn't been. Is that why you're here? That unholy business?"

I said it was, and gave her a look at the license photostat.

She blinked at it. "Why would a private investigator be interested, after all this time? My God, don't tell me something's happened to...the person who was threatened?"

"No. Confidential matter, Ms. Bowers."

"You realize I can't tell you the person's name?"

"That isn't one of my questions. Do you mind talking about the incident?"

Several seconds ticked away. She seemed about to decline, then changed her mind. "I suppose not," she said. "But you'll have to make it brief. I have duties."

"As brief as I can. What Joe Lenihan wrote on his blog is essentially what happened that day?"

"*Exactly* what happened. I'm never likely to forget what that dreadful little man said and did before he died."

"The threat was just as Lenihan quoted it?"

"Word for word," Ms. Bowers said. "I have a very good memory. Too good in that case."

"Would you say Vok was in his right mind at the time?"

"Right mind? I doubt that man was ever in his right mind."

"So you don't think what he said had any sort of factual basis."

"Well, *he* believed every single word. Actually believed he'd made a pact with the devil. Oh, he was one of them, all right. You should have seen his face. His eyes…I swear they glowed like fire the whole time. Brrr. Gives me chills just thinking about it."

"You witnessed him passing the black host?"

"That little black disc? Yes. Vok grabbed the man's arm and pushed the thing into his hand."

"Where did he get it, do you know?"

"It must've been in his shoe."

"Shoe?"

"As weak and near death as he was that morning," Ms. Bowers said, "he kept asking for his shoe, the right shoe. Doctor Adamson, the attending physician, said it couldn't hurt to grant the request if the shoes hadn't been disposed of in the ER clean-up. They hadn't been, and I brought the right one up."

"Was it Doctor Adamson who telephoned…let's call him the victim?"

"Yes. The phone call was Vok's first demand; he made it over and over until the doctor agreed. Dying patients' final requests, no matter how strange, are honored whenever possible."

"What was the victim's reaction to the black host?"

"No reaction, he just stared at it. But his wife…she gasped and turned white as a sheet, I thought she was going to faint when Vok started babbling about Satan."

"Did either of them say anything to him?"

"No."

"Or he say anything more to them?"

"Not a word. The victim shoved the thing into his pocket, grabbed his wife's arm, and hurried her out of there. Vok flatlined less than two minutes after they were gone."

"What about the other man in the room? What can you tell me about him?"

"…I'm sorry?"

"The other man, the one who evidently came to visit Vok."

"I don't know who you mean," Ms. Bowers said. "As far as I'm aware, the patient had no other visitors at all."

"There was no one else in the room at the time?"

"Just the victim and his wife, Vok, and myself. Did Joe tell you there was?"

"No."

"Well, whoever did was mistaken or misinformed."

No, I thought, the individual was making it up. And why would Peter Erskine tell me such a dead-bang lie?

ELEVEN

The main ingredients in detective work are the gathering and interpretation of facts, plus a certain amount of legwork. But instinct also plays a role when you've been at it long enough, a kind of sixth sense that generally comes into play in one of two instances: when an investigation is proceeding well and nearing conclusion, or when the facts indicate you've unintentionally gone or deliberately been led astray. In the latter case, the intuitive feeling is sharp and grows sharper the more attention you pay to it.

Something was wrong here. The kind of wrongness that smacks of manipulation and deceit.

I sat ruminating in the hospital parking lot for the better part of ten minutes. The thinking produced a couple of notions, neither of which I liked worth a damn. Follow-up time. I programmed Erskine's office address into the GPS and pointed the car north.

The address was just off El Camino Real in downtown Menlo Park, a few miles from the Erskines' Atherton home—an older, modernized building that housed three attorneys, an architectural firm, and an orthodontist in addition to Peter Erskine, Financial Advisor. His business name was displayed in fancy gilt script on the frosted glass door. I opened it and went on in.

The woman working on a computer at one of two desks jumped a little at my entrance, as if startled at the appearance of a visitor. She blinked, saw that I was no one she knew, and blinked some more. The professional smile that finally beamed on had a little twitch at one corner.

"Oh, I'm sorry," she said as I shut the door, "I wasn't expecting anyone. May I help you?"

"I'd like a few words with Mr. Erskine."

"I'm sorry," she said again, "he's not here. He left half an hour ago. Did you have an appointment?"

"No appointment. Do you expect him back this afternoon?"

"No, I'm sorry"—for the third time—"not until tomorrow."

"Would you happen to know where he went?"

"I really couldn't say. What was it you wanted to see him about?"

I didn't answer immediately. The anteroom was large and on the posh side, as befitted the type of business Erskine was in: thick carpeting, neatly arranged chrome-and-leather furniture, blandly tasteful prints on the walls. But it had an unused look about it, as if the office were newly opened instead of well established. The young woman's desk contained a blotter, a telephone, and the computer she'd been using; the unoccupied desk had nothing at all on it except a covered computer terminal. One of two closed doors at the rear bore Erskine's name; the second was unmarked.

Except for the twitchy smile, the woman fit well into the posh surroundings. No older than twenty-five, and decoratively attractive in the characterless fashion of so many young people these days: small of stature, shoulder-length hair a thick glossy black, green eyes large, luminous, and canny in an unsophisticated way. Judging from as much as I could see of her body behind the desk, she was eye candy in that respect, too.

"Sir? What was it you wanted to see Mr. Erskine about?"

"Private business matter."

"I see. Well, if you'd like to leave a message or a number where he can reach you...."

"No, thanks, I'll try him at his home. You're Melanie Vinson, is that right?"

"How did you—" The corner of her mouth twitched again. "Did Mr. Erskine tell you my name?"

"Is there a reason he shouldn't have?"

"No." Twitch. "No, of course not."

"Must be an interesting job, working with a stockbroker."

"Yes, it is. Very. And very demanding."
Twitch. "Well. If you're sure you don't want
to leave a message for Mr. Erskine, I have
quite a bit of work to do before I leave for
the day."

"I won't keep you from it, then."

I turned for the door, but before I
reached it she said, "Um, in case you don't
connect with Mr. Erskine at his home,
whom should I say stopped in to see him?"

I gave her my name. It was not the first
time she'd heard it in this office; the smile
twitched all the way off and sharp little
teeth nibbled at her lower lip before she
dropped her gaze to the computer keyboard
and began typing. Not good at hiding her
emotions, the nervous Ms. Vinson.

Why would a man with Peter Erskine's
bizarre problem confide to his secretary/as-
sistant that he'd hired a private investigator?
One more question that needed answering,
and honed even more the sense of manipulation and deceit I felt.

\#

The tall wrought-iron gates were closed across the foot of the Erskines' entrance drive. Locked, too; I got out of the car and tried them. There was an intercom device on one of the pillars. I pushed the pearl button below the speaker, waited, got no response, and tried twice more with the same lack of results. Nobody home. Or nobody home who wanted to be disturbed by a caller no matter who he happened to be.

Before driving away I hauled out the iPhone and called the agency and asked Tamara to do a deeper background check on Peter Erskine. Emphasis on his business practices and personal finances.

"How come?" she asked.

"He lied to me, that's how come, and I haven't been able to find him to ask why." I told her what I'd learned from Ellen Bowers. "No reason for the lie that I can see unless he's got some sort of hidden agenda."

"Such as?"

"I'm not sure yet. That's why I need more data on him, his marriage, his personal life, his business activities. Anything you can dig up that'll give me a better handle on the man."

"Right."

"And while you're at it, run a check on his assistant, Melanie Vinson."

"Ah hah," she said. "So you do think she might be more to him than just office help."

"Could be. She was a lot less professional today than a woman in her position ought to be. She's got something on her mind that doesn't involve stocks and bonds."

"I'll get right on it."

"One more search you can run for me when you have the time. Floyd and Harvey Leno, L-e-n-o, owners of Leno Brothers Painting in Campbell."

"Who're they?"

"Devil cultists...maybe. One of them helped clear out the Voks' apartment the day after he died. I had a little talk with Floyd Leno this afternoon. Nonproductive, but provocative."

"So you want the full package on them, too?"

"Right. Whatever seems relevant."

"Okay. You coming back to the city now?"

"On my way. Not the office, though—home."

"I'll get back to you ASAP."

"It can all wait until tomorrow. Why don't you give yourself a break, go· home early for a change?"

"I *am* home," she said, "right here at my desk. That place on Potrero Hill I pay too much rent for is just where I go to sleep."

TWELVE

Rush-hour traffic heading into the city and on the way up to Diamond Heights added twenty-some minutes to my travel time from Atherton. It was nearly six when I walked into the condo. I'd been there all of five minutes, just enough time to say hello to Emily—Kerry was still at Bates and Carpenter—and open a beer from the fridge when Tamara called.

She'd already run all the backgrounders I'd asked for and compiled fairly substantial dossiers on Peter Erskine, Melanie Vinson, and the Leno brothers. It never takes her long to gather even the most obscure data available on any individual within radar range.

"First off," she said, "the Erskines' marriage isn't so solid after all. Turns out she filed for divorce two and a half years ago, but they reconciled before it ever got to court."

"What prompted the divorce action?"

"Not specified, but I picked up some hints he was having himself a fling and she found out about it."

"You get the woman's name?"

"No. Hush-hush on that. But it probably wasn't Melanie Vinson. She didn't start working for Erskine until sixteen months ago."

"So he strayed at least once."

"At least."

"And his wife won't stand for it happening again. Likely the reconciliation was based on his promise to walk the line and a threat to go through with the divorce if she caught him a second time."

"Right. If she caught him. Doesn't mean he's been Mr. Faithful since, just extra careful."

I said musingly, "Marian Erskine's no dummy, and with all her money she figures to have sound legal representation. Two failed marriages and the third a trophy husband spells pre-nup to me."

"Did to me, too. There was one, I found out that much, but of course I couldn't get the details."

"Usual kind of arrangement, probably. Settlement for X amount of dollars in the event of divorce, with no claim on anything she owned prior to the marriage. I assume that includes the Atherton property?"

"Does. She inherited that along with her Pop's millions."

"What about Erskine's personal finances?"

"Well, he's a lousy stockbroker," Tamara said. "Lost bundles in the market on dubious investments, his own money as well as his clients'. One of the clients threatened him with a lawsuit for fraud. Most of the others quit him quick. He's only got a couple left, just barely hanging on."

"And I take it his wife won't bail him out."

"Did at first, then apparently got tired of the money drain and shut it off. Letting him sink or swim on his own, and he's going down fast."

"I figured as much," I said. "Didn't look as though much if anything was going on in that office of his. The Vinson woman seemed surprised to have somebody walk in unexpectedly."

"Keeps it open and her on salary for appearance sake. Either that, or because he's banging her."

"Uh-huh. Anything more on him I should know?"

"Nothing relevant. Unless the fact that he doesn't drink means something. Won't touch any kind of alcohol, makes a big deal out of it, evidently. My body's my temple kind of thing."

"Either that," I said, "or it's a matter of self discipline. He's the type who doesn't like to lose control."

"Must not like being under his wife's thumb, then. Seems she calls all the shots in the marriage."

"Yes, it does."

"Okay. Melanie Vinson. Erskine didn't hire her because of her stock market savvy or secretarial skills. She didn't have either. Before she went to work for him, she was a saleswoman in a Palo Alto boutique. And before that, a student at San Jose State."

"Any idea whether she met Erskine by applying for the job, or he offered it to her after they met some other way?"

"Nope. Want to bet it was after they met? Party, club, someplace like that."

"No bet."

"Here's the rest of what I pulled up on her," Tamara said. "Born in San Diego, family moved to Milpitas when she was twelve. Father deceased, mother still living. No siblings. Never married. Drama major at S.J.S., wanted to be an actress like about twenty million other kids her age. Small parts in two school plays. Dropped out after a year and a half—lack of funds. Family set up a college fund for her when she was little, but it wasn't substantial enough to carry her through. She wasn't doing well anyway. Not enough talent or ambition and likely poor study habits."

"Any sort of police record?"

"Arrested once for shoplifting a bottle of perfume when she was eighteen. That's all."

"Where does she live?"

"Palo Alto. Expensive apartment building. And her ride is a BMW Z4 sports car. Even secondhand, those babies don't come cheap, and she's had it less than a year." Tamara chuckled and said sardonically, "Erskine must be paying her a pretty hefty salary for sitting around that half dead office of his. I wonder why."

What she'd turned up on the Leno brothers was not particularly illuminating.

Harvey Leno had a minor record—arrested twice, once for public drunkenness, once for aggravated assault, both more than a dozen years past. Married briefly and divorced in the late nineties, no children, no living relatives other than his brother. Floyd Leno was a bachelor with no brushes with the law of any kind. More or less model citizens, on the surface. Paid their bills and taxes on time, made a modest but steady living out of their painting company. Not a whisper of any trafficking with Satanists or other illegal or dubious activities.

Definite dead end there. If I continued my investigation, I would need to scrounge up another lead. If I continued it. The way things were shaping up now, I was pretty sure I wouldn't.

After Tamara and I rang off, I went out onto the balcony—it was a warmish night, clear, myriad lights twinkling in the city panorama spread out below—to do some hard thinking.

So Peter Erskine was a business failure with financial troubles and a sick wife who held tight to the purse strings and kept him on a short leash. What I'd have liked to know were the terms of her will, whether or not he stood to inherit all or some of her fortune if she predeceased him. But as with the conditions of their pre-nup, there was no legal way to find out. Except from her, in answer to a direct question—an unlikely prospect.

The more I thought the more convinced I was that Erskine had a hidden agenda of the nastiest sort. The facts Tamara and I had come up with, the inferences to be drawn from them and from the lies he'd told me, all pointed to it. Some of the details were hazy yet, but the overall design was clear enough.

Vengeance vows, satanic covenants, black masses and black hosts, evil spirits in human form...none of that mattered any more if I was right.

But was all just speculation at this point, without a foundation of proof to support it. If I went to the police with uncorroborated suspicions about a bizarre plot with supernatural overtones, I'd come across as a head case in spite of my long-standing reputation as a reliable investigator.

The only other way to proceed was problematic. I'm always leery of stepping into a volatile situation without hard evidence, but in this case, where it might well mean saving a woman's life, it was my moral duty to run the risk. And do it quick. But

I had to be careful. Very careful. Sticking my oar in could backfire on me and on the agency—leave us wide open to legal action for harassment and defamation of character. We'd been on the receiving end of a similar kind of lawsuit once before, unjustly and maliciously, and if it hadn't been for the plaintiff's sudden demise before the case went to court, the judgment could have gone against us and put us out of business.

All right, then. Tomorrow I would find a way to have a private face-to-face with Marian Erskine, then another with her husband.

I did not have those face-to-face meetings. By then it was too late—too damn late.

Marian Erskine was already dead, of a massive heart attack suffered at her home that same night.

THIRTEEN

It was Tamara who gave me the news when I came into the agency in the morning. She'd decided to see if she could pull up anything more on the Erskines, and there it was. Nothing happens of any newsworthy interest in this world today that isn't reported and disseminated almost immediately on the Internet, and Marian Erskine had been a prominent figure in the Atherton community as well as a major contributor to charitable causes. One more example of the two-edged sword of modern technology: good for business purposes, disastrous for privacy.

People with weak hearts die suddenly all the time. The fatal attacks don't have to be induced by external means, and even when they are, there is no way to prove it without witnesses and/or some sort of physical evidence. Marian Erskine had reportedly been alone when she suffered her coronary, her "bereaved" husband away at a business dinner in Palo Alto. She hadn't died at the Atherton home; she'd been found on the rear terrace alive and unconscious—by none other than Melanie Vinson, who'd made the nine-one-one call—and taken to Peninsula General Hospital where she succumbed at 10:06 p.m. Tragic death by natural causes.

I didn't believe it.

Marian Erskine had been murdered. Cleverly and cold-bloodedly, with malice aforethought.

I said as much to Tamara. And to Jake Runyon, who had arrived a few minutes before I did and been briefed on the situation.

Tamara said, "So you figure the whole thing was a set-up by Erskine to scare his wife into a fatal attack."

"Everything except Vok's shenanigans in the hospital; the revenge vow was genuine enough. Erskine built his plan on that, hatched it after she had her first coronary and barely survived. She might've had another attack as suddenly as the first, but she might also have lived for years. Seems pretty obvious he married her for her money and that he didn't want to wait any longer to gain control of it."

"Assuming she made him beneficiary in her will and didn't write him out after she caught him cheating."

"Sole or major beneficiary, right," I said. "Has to be that way. As far as the plan goes, her credulous belief in the supernatural made it easy for him. A little research was all he needed to manufacture an imitation black host, create the rest of the revenant illusion. I'd be willing to bet he encouraged her cognac drinking, too, whenever the two of them were alone—to weaken her heart even more. Then it was just a matter of escalating the threat. Whatever he arranged to happen last night terrified her enough to do the job."

"Adds up that way for me, too. Jake?"

Runyon nodded his agreement. He's a good man and a good detective, formerly with the Seattle PD and one of the Pacific Northwest's larger private security firms before he went to work for us. He'd moved to San Francisco after his second wife's cancer death, to try to reconcile with his estranged son by his first wife, but the reconciliation hadn't worked out. His way of dealing with lingering grief and loneliness was to throw himself into his work; he put in more hours on the job than even Tamara did.

"But there's one thing I don't get," she said. "Why did Erskine want to hire a detective?"

I said, "I don't think he did."

"You mean it was his wife's idea?"

"That's right. Dominant decision maker, holder of the purse strings—she'd have insisted on it to try to disprove the supernatural explanation. He couldn't talk her out of it without arousing her suspicions, so he pretended it was his idea. And tried his lying best to misdirect me, keep me focused on Vok's alleged connection to a devil cult."

"Who'd he have helping him, impersonating Vok? Vinson's the one who made the nine-one-one call."

"What did the report say she was doing at the Erskine house at that time of night?"

"Delivering some business papers."

"Pretty thin excuse, given that his business is in the dumper."

"Yeah, but she still tried to save Mrs. Erskine's life with the nine-one-one call."

"Maybe not," Runyon said. "Maybe she was supposed to make sure the woman was dead before making the call and misdiagnosed. Even doctors get fooled sometimes."

"So then she could be in it with Erskine. She does the dirty work while he's off establishing an alibi for himself, just in case."

A clutch of frustrated anger made me say, "Dammit, I should have put this together sooner. Gone down there to see her last night instead of waiting. I might have been able to forestall what happened, convince her she was the real target."

Runyon said, "And you might not have been able to do either. Don't blame yourself.

You were on the case less than two days— that's little enough time to wade through misdirection and subterfuge." The calm voice of reason, as usual with him.

"It's still galling. I hate like hell being used."

"Don't we all."

"What bites my ass," Tamara said, "is that Erskine's probably gonna get away with it."

I said, "Not if I have anything to say about it. There has to be a way to expose him."

"What way? There's no proof."

"None yet. Doesn't mean we can't find some."

"How?"

"You could try rattling his cage a little," Runyon said. "Let him know you're on to him, see if you can get him to self-incriminate."

"Pretty difficult to manage if I'm reading him right," I said. "But it'll do for starters."

#

I rang up the Erskine home. No answer. Peter Erskine's cell number next. Straight to voice mail. The message I left made no mention of his wife's death; let him think I hadn't heard about it yet. I said I had uncovered some information about Antanas Vok that he should know about and requested a callback ASAP. If he was checking his messages today, it shouldn't be too long before I heard from him.

An idea occurred to me—a long shot but worth taking a chance on. I went into Tamara's office, asked her to find out which fire department's emergency response team had answered Melanie Vinson's nine-one-one call. And if possible, the name or names of the individuals manning the EMT units, as well as the names of the ER doctors at Peninsula General who'd attended to Marian Erskine.

Tall order, and only partially successful. No luck on IDing the ER doctors. But it was the Menlo Fire Protection District that served Atherton and its Station 4 had responded with an Advanced Life Support Engine manned by a fireman and a licensed paramedic. Their names were also unavailable, but I ought to be able to find that out by a visit to Station 4.

It was past noon, and the office routine was wearing on me, when Peter Erskine returned my call. He said in slow, sepulchral tones, "I'm afraid I have terrible news. My wife passed away last night. Her poor heart finally gave out."

"Yes," I said, "I just heard. My condolences."

"Thank you. It wasn't unexpected—she had a severe coronary three months ago—but I'm still in shock."

"Sure you are. She was alone at the time, I understand."

"Yes, and I blame myself for that. I had a business dinner scheduled in Palo Alto and Marian insisted I go. She said she'd be all right, she'd keep a pistol close at hand in case that Vok crazy showed up again."

"Did he?"

"I don't know. How would I know? There was no sign of anyone on the grounds." Erskine sighed heavily. "I wish to God I'd stayed home. I may have been able to save her if I'd been there when it happened."

"Or if your assistant had gotten there a little sooner."

"Yes. It was too late by then. Neither the paramedics nor the hospital ER doctors could do anything to revive her."

"How did Ms. Vinson happen to come to your home?"

"Miscommunication between us," Erskine said. "She brought some documents she'd been working on, thinking I needed them right away and that I'd be home. I completely forgot to tell her about the business dinner."

I said, "Why did she go around to the back terrace? That's where she found your wife, isn't it?"

"All the lights were on and there was no answer to the bell. My dear Marian was just lying there."

My dear Marian. Jesus. "And Ms. Vinson assumed she was already dead."

"She couldn't find a pulse and Marian didn't seem to be breathing."

"Big mistake on her part."

"Mistake?" Pause. "No, I can't fault her for that. She's had no medical training, doesn't know CPR."

"How come the gates were open, if she wasn't expected?"

"…The gates?"

"She couldn't have driven onto the property otherwise. They open by remote control, so they must've been unlocked."

Longer pause this time, while he manufactured an answer. "You're right, of course," he said when he had one. "I must have released the lock button too soon after I drove out."

"I'd have thought you'd be more careful, under the circumstances."

"I should've been, yes. But locked gates didn't prevent that Vok lunatic from getting onto the property before."

"So it's a good possibility he did show up again last night. That he was the cause of your wife's attack."

"I suppose that's possible. But I'm the one he's after."

"Maybe he changed his tactics. Went after her instead."

"Why would he do that?"

"Could be she was a target too. All along."

"I don't believe that." Stiffly, warily now. "No."

"In any case," I said, "another of those sudden appearances would have terrified her. And we both know how effective a weapon fear can be. As powerful and deadly a weapon as a gun or a knife."

No response for several beats. Then, "But we don't know he came again last night, do we."

"Did your wife have the pistol in her possession when Ms. Vinson found her?"

"The pistol? No, it was on the table near where she fell."

"Fired?"

"No." Pause. "You've kept all that Marian and I told you about Vok and the devil worshippers in confidence, haven't you?"

"Of course. You didn't tell the authorities about it, either, I take it."

"Hardly. This is a painful enough time for me. If the media got hold of that crazy business…well, you understand."

"All too well," I said.

Erskine made a tight little throat-clearing sound. "Why did you call me? Something to do with your investigation?"

"That's right. I picked up a pretty good lead. A couple of strangers showed up and cleaned out the Voks' apartment the morning after Vok died. Creepy types, according to the building manager."

"Members of that damned devil cult."

"If there is a devil cult."

"There has to be. Did you get their names?"

"Not yet. You want me to keep working on it?

He was ready for that one. "Certainly. Why wouldn't I? As far as I know my life is still in danger."

"Sure it is." Clever bastard, all right. Keep up the pretense a while longer, let me run around chasing devil cultists that had nothing to do with him, then find a way to ease me out of the picture.

"I can't talk any more right now," he said, "I'm due at the funeral home to make burial arrangements."

"One thing before you go. Whose decision was it to hire a detective, yours or your wife's?"

"What? Why do you want to know that?"

"Required for our files. Yours or your wife's?"

"Mine," Erskine said, and immediately broke the connection.

Okay. So I'd rattled his cage as much as I thought was wise at this point. He was perceptive as well as cunning; he'd gotten the message that I was on to him. It wouldn't worry him much right now—he was too sure of himself and the invincibility of his plan—but it might make him a little more vulnerable next time I talked to him. I would not be nearly as subtle when I did.

Still, my gut feeling was that it would take a lot more than words to break Peter Erskine. If he could be broken at all.

FOURTEEN

Menlo Fire Station #4 was a small building
that housed a modern pumper and the Advanced Life Support vehicle. Originally it
must have been solid brick, in keeping with
its attractive upscale surroundings, but like
so many brick structures that had survived
the devastating Loma Prieta earthquake in
'89, it had been redesigned and rebuilt to
conform to seismic safety regulations. According to Tamara's search, it was manned
24/7 by a captain and two firefighters working shifts of seventy-two hours on, seventy-
two hours off, and the trio working today
were the same three who been on duty last
night.

My investigator's license and mention
of the fact that I was employed by Peter Erskine got me an audience with the captain.
He was a little leery of me at first, until I

assured him that I was not there to question his team's response time and life-saving efforts; everybody these days, especially public servants, is litigation-fearful and prickly because of it. Mr. Erskine, I explained, was only interested in knowing if his wife had been conscious at any time while she was being stabilized and/or during her transport to Peninsula General, and if so, if she'd said anything—any last words that might be a comfort to him. I don't like lying to people, particularly lies of this sort, but you do what you have to do in the interest of justice.

The captain didn't seem to find the request unusual. He said Mrs. Erskine had been conscious briefly, but couldn't tell me if she'd spoken. That information would have to come from the other two members of the team, and they were currently out on a call. I was welcome to wait for their return.

The wait lasted nearly an hour and a half. When the ALS unit finally pulled in, I had to hang on another fifteen minutes while they did some clean-up work on the engine. It was four o'clock by then. If the two firefighters had nothing to tell me, I'd head over to Peninsula General. The evening-shift ER personnel would have come on duty and I might be able to convince a doctor or nurse who had attended Marian Erskine to talk to me.

But it didn't come to that. The firefighters were cooperative, and the licensed paramedic, a young, linebacker-size Latino named Tejada, told me what I wanted to know.

"The woman was conscious, yes," he said, "but only for a minute or so as I was stabilizing her. She was in very bad shape. Frankly I was surprised she survived the ride to the hospital."

"Did she say anything?"

"Yes, but it didn't make too much sense."

"To me, either," the other firefighter said. He was an older man, a red-haired Irishman named Reilly. "Delirious mumblings."

"Can either of you recall what it was she said?"

"Something about shooting somebody, wasn't it, Alex?"

Tejada dipped his chin. "Sounded like 'I shot him three times but he wouldn't fall down, he just kept coming at me.' "

I made an effort to keep my expression blank so they couldn't tell how much significance those words held for me. "Is that all?"

"All that was coherent."

"Was there a gun anywhere near her when you got there?"

"A gun? No."

"Could one have been on a nearby table, maybe?"

Reilly said, "No gun. We'd've seen it if there was, after what she said about shooting somebody."

I thanked them and was about to leave when Tejada said, "You know, I just remembered something else she said. One word, just before she went under for good."

"What word?"

"Reverend."

"Sure that's what it was?"

"Pretty sure." He shook his head sadly and crossed himself. "Knew she was dying, poor lady. Asking for a padre."

No, I thought as I went out to the car, she hadn't been asking for a padre. Tejada had misheard: the last word spoken by Marian Erskine hadn't been "reverend."

It had been "revenant."

#

So now I had a pretty good idea of how they'd worked it last night. Manufacture enough raw terror with the right kind of supernatural trappings and you can practically guarantee a weak heart will stop beating without ever laying a hand on the victim. Neat, clean, sadistically bloodless—the so-called perfect crime.

Like hell it was.

Prod Erskine some more now? I decided against it. Marian Erskine's last words were a piece of evidence against him, but only a small piece. Push him too far too soon, even if I made no direct accusation, and he was liable to sic a lawyer on me.

Better idea: He was the strong link, so go after the potential weak link instead.

Melanie Vinson.

If my take on her was accurate, she was a long way from being a mental giant—an easily manipulated follower who'd gone along with the murder scheme out of greed or love or a combination of both. In over her head, and at least a little scared; her twitchiness yesterday in Erskine's office, on the eve of her part in delivering the death-blow, suggested that.

Fear can be a weapon in serving justice, too, if you use it effectively. Turn hers back on her and it might well crack her wide open. And if she cracked, the odds were good she'd take Erskine down to save herself.

FIFTEEN

The offices of Peter Erskine, Financial Advisor were locked up tight. I hadn't expected otherwise, but the building was on my way out of Menlo Park and I had nothing to lose but a few minutes by stopping there first. I programmed Melanie Vinson's home address into the GPS, followed the disembodied voice's directions into Palo Alto and through a maze of residential streets not far from the Stanford University campus.

It was after five o'clock and already dark when the voice told me I'd arrived at my destination—a block of facing rows of townhouse-style apartments extending back from the street in the shape of a broad horseshoe. Not a new complex, but well maintained, in a neighborhood so thick with shade trees it had a bucolic atmosphere. I'd seen modern rent/lease places like this before, often enough to know that there would be a courtyard with a communal swimming pool and recreation area in the middle of the two wings. Driveways angled up adjacent to each wing, along which were shedlike structures where the tenants parked their cars.

I wedged mine into a spot at the curb across the street. Before I got out, I transferred the voice-activated tape recorder I keep in the glove compartment into my coat pocket. The night was clouding up and a cold wind had begun to blow; I pulled up the collar on my suit coat as I followed a walkway into an open foyer in the front curve of the horseshoe. Melanie Vinson occupied apartment number eleven; I rang the bell—once, twice, three times, leaning on it the last two. No response. Not home or ducking visitors if she was.

Thanks to Tamara, I had Vinson's landline and cell numbers written down in my notebook. Landline first: four rings, and an answering machine with one of those smart-ass-cute "you know what to do at the beep" messages kicked in. I clicked off before the beep sounded and tried the cell number: straight to voice mail.

Damn. Now what?

I went back outside. Crosswise paths led to the driveways along both sides. On impulse I followed the one that hooked around to the right, where the parking space for Vinson's apartment would be. Nightlights shone brightly back there, both inside and outside the covered parking structure. Each slant-in space had a unit number spray-painted on the tarmac. And tucked into number eleven was a sleek black BMW Z4 sports car with a personalized license plate: MELSBBY. Mel's Baby. Mel for Melanie.

So either she was home and avoiding calls and callers, or more likely, she'd gone off with somebody. Erskine, probably. They had to be feeling good about the way the plan had gone, considering themselves inviolate despite my suspicions. Why not get together and celebrate the successful elimination of the woman who'd stood in the way of their lust for wealth, the sick woman who'd never done either of them any harm?

There was nobody in the parking area. I made sure of that, then moved in alongside the BMW to the driver's door. Locked— naturally. I bent to peer through the window, but the overhead light was not strong enough to give me a clear look inside. About all I could make out was that neither of the bucket seats had anything on them.

I straightened up. More than a few people have a tendency to lose or misplace their car keys, or leave them in the ignition and then snap-lock the door when they get out, and as a safeguard some hide a spare key inside one of those little magnetized cases somewhere on the vehicle. If Melanie Vinson was one of them....

I eased around the front of the BMW, bending low to run my fingers behind the license plate and then along the underside of the bumper from one end to the other. All I felt was grit. I'd just started on the frame beneath the front fender and driver's side door panels when headlights splashed in along the driveway from the street.

I dropped to one knee and stayed there, in close to the car. Neither the beams nor the incoming vehicle reached as far as the number eleven space; they angled into one closer to the street and immediately went dark. A man and a woman got out, chattering to each other, and drifted away toward a side entrance to the building wing. I didn't raise up until I heard a door slam over there.

There was nothing along the BMW's underbelly on this side, nothing under or inside the rear bumper. But then I got lucky. My fingers touched metal, felt the little square shape clipped up inside the rear wheel well on the passenger side.

I tugged the case loose. The spare key was inside. I fished it out, replaced the case where I'd found it. The spare had a couple of remote buttons on it, but I wasn't familiar with this make and model and had no idea if the remote made beeping sounds when you used it; some vehicles of this vintage operated that way. So I unlocked the driver's door with the key.

Quickly I wedged myself in under the wheel to cut off the interior light. Tight fit—I had a lot of pounds and girth on Melanie Vinson—but I could maneuver all right without adjusting the seat control.

The console storage compartment was locked, but the spare key opened that, too. I used my pencil flash to fast-check the contents. Registration slip, insurance card, half full package of menthol coffin nails, unopened packets of Kleenex and tampons…nothing to hold my attention. The slender pockets in both doors were empty. I squeezed out again, levered the driver's seat forward so I could look behind it and the one on the passenger side. The only items on the floor were a couple of empty Starbuck's coffee containers and some wadded-up tissues.

I pushed the seat back in place, located and freed the trunk release before shutting the door. Around to the rear, then, to lift the trunk lid.

There was one item on the carpeted floor inside: a large, bulky laundry sack closed at the top by a drawstring. I loosened the string, widened the opening to see what was inside the bag.

Antanas Vok was inside the bag.

Shabby, ripped, dirt-caked black suit that stank of rotting meat. Stained white shirt. Old, dirty black shoes. Wide-brimmed black slouch hat. Realistic theatrical mask with dark bushy eyebrows and Van Dyke beard glued on, the malleable latex material coated with some sort of luminous paint to give it an eerie glow in the dark. A pair of black gloves, fingers and thumbs on each painted to resemble skeletal hands.

There was a handgun, too, a .32 caliber Smith & Wesson five-shot revolver. I picked it up by the trigger guard, using the back of my index finger, and sniffed the barrel. Fired recently. With a couple of knuckles I broke the weapon to peer at the chambers. Three empty shells, two loaded ones. And all of them would be blanks. *I shot him three times but he wouldn't fall down, he just kept coming at me.* Yeah, blanks.

No surprises in any of this. Vinson had to have been the one impersonating Vok; Erskine was too smart to bring a third party into the scheme. She was the right height, the same approximate size. With that outfit and the mask on, and the hat pulled down low over her forehead, she'd have passed easily for a middle-aged man. Plus she'd had acting experience, enough to pull off the menacing act with Erskine's help and guidance.

I stuffed everything back into the sack, retightened the drawstring, then lifted the bag out. I couldn't risk leaving it here without constant surveillance on the BMW; she might decide, or Erskine might tell her, to make it all disappear. I closed the trunk, relocked the driver's door, and pocketed the key in case in became necessary to return the sack at some point. Then I swung it up over my shoulder and quick-stepped down the empty driveway.

Two cars passed on my way to where I'd parked mine, but so far as I could tell none of the occupants paid any attention to me. Tenants hauling their laundry to a nearby Laundromat were common sights in almost any neighborhood. Just the same, I felt an easing of tension once the bag was locked away in the trunk.

#

What had taken place at the Erskine home last night was clear now. It must have gone something like this:

In costume Vinson slips onto the property same as the other times, catches Marian Erskine unaware inside the house or already sitting out on the terrace, advances on her in a threatening manner. Victim has the gun in hand or close to hand, fires three of what she believes are live rounds. Vinson keeps coming, the way a genuine revenant would. And in horror and sudden savage pain, down goes Marian Erskine.

Then Vinson makes her first mistake. She's supposed to be certain the victim is dead before calling nine-one-one, but haste and nervousness cause her to misdiagnose; she doesn't realize until the firefighters arrive that Mrs. Erskine is still alive. Bad moment for her, but she manages to hang onto her nerve. By then she's retrieved the gun, gone to wherever she stashed her regular clothing, changed, loaded the costume and weapon into the laundry bag, and hid the bag in the trunk of her car.

Her second mistake was leaving the bag there. Maybe she was supposed to get rid of the contents somewhere, or at least hide the revolver inside her apartment until she could return it to Erskine. Or maybe she just didn't think there was any hurry. From her perspective, no one had any reason to search her car.

I had a case now against the two of them: my testimony, Marian Erskine's dying words, the array of sure to be fingerprint-laden evidence in the sack. But it was by no means conclusive, not where a

wealthy Atherton citizen and allegedly bereaved widower was concerned. Enough,
maybe, to convince the local authorities to
mount an investigation, but just as likely
not. I needed more solid proof.

So?

Couple of options. Pack it in for the
day, go home to my family, and take steps
tomorrow to see Melanie Vinson alone and
try to crack her as I'd originally intended.
Or stay put for a while in the hope that
she'd return at a reasonable hour and I could
brace her tonight. If she was with Erskine
and he went into her townhouse with her,
all the better. I liked the prospect of bracing
the two of them together in a place he had
no good reason for being the day after his
wife's death, catching them off guard, making an effort to provoke her if not him into
an incriminating slip with the tape recorder
running. I'd settle for Vinson alone, but it
was Erskine I most wanted to confront.

The second option, then. I dislike stake-
outs after sitting through scores of them
over the years, but I was angry and deter-

mined enough to tolerate one more of short duration. And I had a good vantage point from here, a clear look at the front entrance to the complex. Seven-thirty now. Give it a couple of hours at least.

I called Kerry to tell her I'd be home late, then tried to make myself comfortable. Good luck with that, in Tamara's vernacular. My aging body tends to cramp up if I sit more than a few minutes in any one position, and shifting around only increases the pressure on my tailbone. I had to get out twice and take short walks in the cold wind to stretch the kinks out of my lower back.

Eight-thirty, nine o'clock. A few cars arrived and parked on the street or pulled into the nearside driveway, and half a dozen people went in through the front entrance. None of them was Vinson or Erskine.

Hunger pangs increased my discomfort. I hadn't eaten since a light lunch. In the old days I kept a bunch of light snacks—potato chips, peanut butter crackers, cookies—in the car for unplanned-for downtime such as this, but now that I did little field work and had pretty much given up junk food for health reasons, I no longer bothered to stock up. All I found when I rummaged around in the glove box was one of the dinky little energy bars Emily is fond of. Apricot, except it didn't taste much like apricot; it tasted like chewy cardboard and only made me hungrier.

Nine-thirty.

Quarter of ten.

The hell with it. It had been a long day, I was tired and stiff and cold as well as hungry, and it was a forty-some mile drive back to the city. No sense in pushing myself past a sensible limit. Start fresh tomorrow.

I got the engine going and headed for home.

SIXTEEN

But home was not where I went. I took an impulsive and ill-advised detour instead.

I was on Page Mill Road, nearing the intersection with Highway 280, when the thought began to nag at me that Erskine might have taken Vinson home with him. Would the son of a bitch be that bold, that callous? Sure he would. Dinner first, maybe, someplace where they weren't known, then a return to the scene of the crime to finish up their celebration. No risk to him; he'd committed the perfect murder, hadn't he? It wasn't likely any of the neighbors would notice them arriving, but if they were spotted and the fact was later mentioned to him, why, he'd just say she was helping put his wife's affairs in order, or comforting him in his time of need. He wouldn't give much of a damn what the neighbors thought anyway.

Couldn't hurt to swing by his house, could it? It was more or less on the way, a round trip detour off 280 of only a few miles. If the place was dark I needn't stop; if it showed lights, I could ring the bell, late as it was, and see if I could get him to let me in—feed him a story about being on my way back from San Jose where I'd uncovered some information about the Leno brothers. Might just work. Then what I could do was make it plain, without actually accusing him, that I had the entire scheme figured. Escalate the war of nerves—the Javert treatment. If Vinson was there and stashed someplace where she could listen to the conversation, it might scare her enough so she'd be easier to crack when I tackled her alone.

It was not much of an idea, a product of weariness, frustration, and a compulsive need to confront Erskine, but I could not talk myself out of it. When the Atherton exit came up, I turned off and let the disembodied voice guide me through a series of curves and turns to the Erskine property.

No lights showed at the front of the house, but the gates at the foot of the drive were wide open. Funny. Whether he was home or not, why hadn't he bothered to close them?

I turned in between them for a better view. Amber-colored ground lanterns illuminated the driveway; more of the same glowed like stationary fireflies all across the grounds. I couldn't tell from here whether or not there were any lighted windows at the sides or rear of the house. Except for the nightlights, the darkness was thick with restless shadows. Overhead, fast-moving clouds driven by high altitude winds hid the stars and the sickle moon except for brief breaks in the leaden canopy.

Well?

Well, I'd come this far. Go on up and ring the bell and let's see what happens.

I drove through the gates and up the drive. Halfway along, where the shrubbery thinned out, I could see part of the lantern-lit path that led to the summerhouse, a darkened hulk against the screen of evergreens. A faint yellowish sheen lay over a portion of the side terrace: drapes open in the sun room, one or more lights burning inside.

A light-colored Corvette drawn up on the white-pebble parking area confirmed that at least Erskine was here. I rolled up next to it, doused the headlamps. When I got out, I stepped over to the Corvette and laid a hand on its hood. Warm. Wherever he'd been tonight he hadn't been home long.

I crossed slowly to the porch. The night's silence was broken only by wind-rattle in trees and shrubbery; there were no sounds that I could make out inside the house. If Vinson was here with him, they were somewhere at the rear—in bed together, like as not.

I put my finger on the bell, but I didn't push it. There was tension in me all of a sudden; the skin across my neck and shoulders had begun to pull and prickle. Another of those sixth-sense feelings of wrongness, sudden this time, setting off the silent danger alarm inside my head.

For some seconds I stood still, listening, looking around. Still quiet inside the house, nothing visibly or aurally changed out here. But the feeling remained strong just the same. Strong enough to prod me off the porch, over onto a lighted path that led around on the terraced side.

I hadn't gone more than a few steps when the woman screamed.

The cry came from outside the house, toward the rear—a high-pitched shriek that shattered the stillness and brought me up short, raised the hairs on the back of my neck.

Confusion of sounds then: garbled yells, scrapings and scufflings, a sharp metallic clatter as of a wrought-iron table or chair knocked over onto the terrace bricks. The woman screeched again, terrified words this time that carried distinctly on the wind.

"Peter, who...oh God, this can't be happening!"

Another scraping noise, the pop of shattering glass.

The woman: "What're you doing? Why are you—? No! *No, don't—!*"

Running footfalls. And then the sudden crack of a gun, a large caliber weapon that sent echoes hammering through the darkness.

I had taken a couple of steps toward the corner; the report twisted me around, sent me running back to the car. Only a damn fool rushes unarmed into an unknown, firearms-deadly situation. I dragged the car door open, leaned in to release the hidden compartment under the dash, yanked out the snub-nosed Colt Bodyguard I keep in there for emergencies, and ran back toward the far side of the house.

More sounds battered the night, a male voice now, yelling something I couldn't understand.

Near the corner I slowed, holding the .38 up next to my ear, drawing in close to the sweet-smelling shrubbery that grew there; charge out into the open and you're a target even on a dark night. Before I could get my head around for a clear look, the yelling morphed into a kind of panicked wail. Other cries followed it, diminishing. Man on the run, howling like a banshee.

I stepped out away from the shrubbery with the revolver leveled. A rent in the cloud cover opened just then, letting enough starlight and moonshine leak through to bathe the yard in faint luminescence. In the two or three beats before the tear closed, I had a glimpse of what seemed to be two figures stumbling up the steps into the summerhouse, one clinging to the other from behind. False impression, my old eyes playing tricks. Only one figure had fused into the black-dark inside—Erskine, still emitting that half-crazed wail.

The night was shadow-haunted again as I ran in a crouch toward the side terrace. I did not see the woman until I was only a few feet from where she lay in a dip in the lawn beyond the bricks, face down with both arms outflung.

I veered that way, dropped to one knee beside her—and my stomach churned even though I was braced for the worst. The slug from the shot I'd heard had opened up the back of her head just above the neck; spatters of blood and bone and brain matter matted her black hair. Melanie Vinson. I did not need to touch her to verify it.

Over in the summerhouse, the wailing stopped and Erskine's voice bellowed, "You can't force me this time, I won't let you! Go back where you came from, go to hell!" Then the gun banged loud again.

I ducked instinctively, but the round hadn't been directed my way. Almost immediately, there was another outburst from Erskine in the summerhouse darkness, rising above the noises made by the wind. "Not me, goddamn you, not me, not me!"

The cries were soaked in such visceral terror they drove me up onto my feet, sideways to the path that led over there. Erskine spewed something else, but the wind gusted just then and tore away the sense of it. The wildly flailing tree branches and running clouds created a gyrating dance of shadows, surreal, like images in a madman's dream.

And the gun went off a third time.

I was looking straight at the summerhouse and I saw the muzzle flash, saw the shape of him as he went down. An instant later, I saw something else, or thought I did—a different kind of flare, so brief it was like a subliminal image of a comet's tail streaking across the night sky. Gone in an eyeblink, if it had ever been there in the first place.

I stepped farther away from the path, to keep out of the amber glow from the lanterns. But nothing else happened. Silence, now, inside the summerhouse. The only sounds anywhere were the whistles and moans of the wind and the rattling tree branches.

I kept on going, slow, getting the pencil flash out of my pocket with my left hand as I went. At the summerhouse steps I paused again to listen—still nothing to hear—and then climbed them carefully with the .38 extended.

Needless precaution. What was left of Peter Erskine lay on the floor next to one of the chaise lounges, his head as much a bloody mess as Melanie Vinson's, the weapon he'd used, a .357 Magnum, clutched in one hand. The pencil light showed something else, too: scratches on his neck and back, rips in his shirt in half a dozen places.

And no one else was there.

SEVENTEEN

The official police verdict, based on what I'd witnessed that night and on the evidence corroborating my suspicions about Marian Erskine's fatal coronary, was murder-suicide. Of course.

That was my verdict, too. Of course.

Peter Erskine had had a psychotic break, brought on by factors that could only be guessed at: fear of punishment for the murder of his wife, uncontrollable rage against his co-conspirator, an unstable psychological makeup. He'd killed Melanie Vinson because she wanted more money, or had threatened him in some way, or for no rational reason at all—love and lust flaring into sudden hatred, sudden violence. Then he'd cracked up completely, run screaming to the summerhouse, and blew himself away on the second try.

He'd been the only one in there, all three bullets fired had come from his Magnum, and the only fingerprints found on the weapon were his. It was inconceivable that another person could have been on the property, chased him after he shot the woman, dodged the first bullet, taken the weapon away and used it on Erskine, then escaped without my seeing any sign of him. The figure that had seemed to be clinging to Erskine was simply a distortion of shadows created by the scudding clouds and the wind-tossed evergreens. The torn shirt and the scratches on his back and neck had been done by Melanie Vinson during the struggle I'd heard on the terrace. The first shot from inside the summerhouse had been aimed at himself, only he'd been in such a state he'd missed completely; that slug had been found lodged in one of the support posts. And the words I'd heard him shouting were nothing more than deranged babblings.

The other explanation that crawled into my head, the supernatural one, I dismissed immediately as absurd. And did not mention to anybody, not even Tamara and Jake Runyon. Antanas Vok's spirit had returned after all to exact vengeance by means of assault and demonic possession? Erskine's blatant, contemptuous mockery of the powers of darkness had provoked sufficient wrath to permit it to happen? No. *Hell*, no. The only demons at work that night were the ones that existed inside Peter Erskine's psyche.

Never mind that a ruthless control freak who had put together a murder plan requiring cold, steel-nerved calculation is about as unlikely a candidate for mental breakdown and willful self-destruction as there is. Never mind that he believed he'd gotten away with it, and therefore had fifteen million reasons to maintain his emotional balance and to go on living. Never mind that the bullet in the support post had been at belt level, opposite where he'd been standing, as if he had fired not at himself but at someone or something in front of him. Never mind that neither skin nor blood had been found under Melanie Vinson's fingernails. And never mind the subliminal flare I thought I'd seen just after the second shot in the summerhouse; it was either my imagination or a retinal anomaly, an afterimage of the gun flash. There are always inconsistencies, unanswerable questions in cases like this. People go off the deep end all the time, for no clear-cut reasons. I'd seen it happen before, on more than one occasion.

Murder-suicide, period.

Because I can't, I won't believe the dead can harm the living in any way for any purpose.

Because there is no such thing as a revenant.